Renard Falca

Lord Poverty's Assets

A Comedy Drama in Four Acts

Renard Falca

Lord Poverty's Assets
A Comedy Drama in Four Acts

ISBN/EAN: 9783744784191

Printed in Europe, USA, Canada, Australia, Japan

Cover: Foto ©Andreas Hilbeck / pixelio.de

More available books at **www.hansebooks.com**

LORD
POVERTY'S ASSETS

A COMEDY-DRAMA

In Four Acts

By RENARD FALCA.

The Persons of the Play.

LORD COURTLAND POVERTY.
JONATHAN RUSHFOOT.
JOHN RANDOLPH ROBINS JR. (Jack).
GEORGE MABY.
SIGNIOR SIRAO.
MR. GOWER.
MAXEY.
TAYLOR.
MRS. SMILE.
MRS. MABY.
HELEN RUSHFOOT (her sister).
EFFIE REVERE.
MISS BENSON.
BULLOCK.

Messenger, Reporters, Constable
etc. etc.

LORD POVERTY'S ASSETS

Time: 'During discussion of the Arbitration Treaty in the United States Senate.

THE FIRST ACT.

The Scene is a room, in apartment on ground floor of Maby Building, Dorchester Oaks, England. An apartment temporarily occupied by the Anglo-American Arbitration League.
Signor Sirao has possession of the room, for the purpose of exhibiting " Van Elfins 'Peace." On the right is a door leading into reception room, that communicates, it is supposed, with large room used as a banqueting hall, and that in turn, leads into ball room. Over the door hangs a portiere, drawn aside. On the left is an arched entrance opening, it is supposed, into small hall that communicates with main hall of building. The reception room to the right also communicates, it is supposed, with small hall. On the left is a door leading, it is supposed into empty room. Facing the audience is a large painting in massive gilt frame. The canvas is concealed by rich crimson curtains, drawn, and fastened by locked clasps. Above the painting is a row of gas jets with reflectors to illuminate the canvas. To the right of large painting hang portraits of George Washington and Richard Olney, and to the left, portraits of George the Third and Lord Salisbury. American and English colors decorate the walls. Tables chairs, large swivelled mirror, &c., &c., are on the scene. Mrs. Smile appears at right, stands for a moment as though addressing some one behind her. Clapping of hands, and other evidences of applause, heard behind the scene. Enters Mrs. Smile.
Mrs. Smile. — (*A tall, handsome, well bred woman about thirty two; with charming manner, but at heart, a jealous, revengeful hypocrite; stopping at nothing to accomplish her purpose.*) The violence of colonel Rushfoot's, oratory

is deafning! Come! Let us see the painting. (*Gower appears at entrance.*) Sirao will be here in a moment to draw the curtains. Such screaching! (*Enters* Gower).

Gower. – (*A substantial, good looking Englishman of forty*). But there's sense in the colonel's noise.

Mrs. Smile. -- Possibly. (Yankee Doodle *heard behind scene.*)

Gower. — (*Looks toward painting.*) The colonel is a fine chap. He's for arbitration between England and the States.

Mrs. Smile.— (*Laughs ironically.*) Why Gordon, are you too suffering with Yankee smite?

Gower. — (*Earnestly.*) I'm for arbitration with our American cousins.

Mrs. Smile. — Ha! ha! ha! This American cousin epidemic may elect Maby to parliament.

Gower. — Quite so.

Mrs. Smile. — (*Assertively.*) He was beaten at the last election.

Gower. — Ah! but this is a bye-election.

Mrs. Smile. — (*With spirit.*) I wish I were a man!

Gower. — I don't, considering the fact that I'm soon to marry you.

Mrs. Smile. — (*Without heeding Gowers' last remark.*) I'ed tell the members of the Anglo-American Arbitration League, that they were fools!

Gower (*Smiling*). — They might be uncivil and contradict you.

Mrs. Smile. — Who organized this league, who's paid ten thousand pounds for this painting (*Pointing to Painting*) that on the nineteenth, the league accepts amid imposing ceremonies—and more Yankee Doodle —and cheers for Uncle Sam and Arbitration? George Maby! and why? He wants a seat in parliament— this English husband of Mrs. Rushfoot—Maby, daughter of the great Yankee mine owner, and millionaire, but once ha! ha! ha!— a Texas cow-boy.

Gower. — Here, here, here! (*Laughs*).

Mrs. Smile. — Who of late has been giving grand dinners, proclaiming her feasts aloud, like the farmer from his barn door with a peck of corn under his arm, who calls—chick, chick, chick. — Mrs. Rushfoot—Maby! (*Laughs*). How the society electors, the social pullets, the old hens and ogleing cocks spread their wings and run with cackling joy, when they hear chick, chick, chick from the porch of Devon House. Soon Dorchester Oaks will be summoned to Madam Maby's generous spreads to the tune of Yankee Doodle. Does this woman throw her vulgar revenue about her for nothing? No! she has decreed for her English husband a parliamentary career. (*Laughs*.) Who knows? She may yet buy him a coronet. And do you know, these people have invited His Royal Highness, the Prince of Wales to their Celebration? Such audacity!

Gower. — By Jove Lizzie, if you were a man.

Mrs. Smile (*Interrupting*). — I'd thwart the designs of this Yankee woman.

Gower. — But she's fond of you.

Mrs. Smile. — She ought to be. At school in London, I loved her as a sister, and I continued to love her up to the day of my husbands bankruptcy, three months before his death. See how she has repaid my devotion! By a nod, she could have snatched him from the vortex of insolvency. My tears moved her not. She had a motive!

Gower. — A motive?

Mrs. Smile. — Yes! The social life of Dorchester Oaks, was too circumscribed for her to share its first honors with even her dearest friend. (*Laughing*.) How I do rave when I think!

Gower (*Goes to right; looks into drawing room*). — That's right, forget it.

Mrs. Smile. — (*Aside.*) Yes, when I'm your wife and am again in a social position to jostle Mrs. Moneybags with a strong elbow.

Gower. — Hallo! here's Lord Poverty surrounded by the—

Mrs. Smile.—(*Interrupting.*) Yankees of Devon House.

Gower. — By the Rushfoots and the Mabys.   He's got his top coat on.   Can it be possible.

Mrs. Smile. — (*Interrupting*). What ?

Gower. — That he's going home ?

Mrs. Smile. — Ha, ha, ha!   Not while there's any waltzing in the neighborhood.

Gower. - He's a fine waltzer.

Mrs. Smile. — Yes, and he plays the picolo. (*Laughs.*) The Rushfoots admire him no doubt, because of his grace and musical talents.

Gower. — Especially the latter.   Their admiration for the picalo—

Mrs. Smile. — (*Interrupting*). Overcomes their supreme repugnance to his title, and the accident of his high birth. (*Both Laugh*).

Gower. — By the way, Helen Rushfoot is pretty.

Mrs. Smile. — (*Indifferently.*) Yes, but impertinant and slangy.

Gower. — And rich.

Mrs. Smile. — Ten thousand a year in her own right.

Gower. - The latter fact accounts for Poverty's break with the new organist.

Mrs. Smile. — Miss Revere?

Gower. — Yes, he's given her up.

Mrs. Smile. — Nonsense! (*Looks at Gower.*) What do you suppose ! last Wednesday evening at twilight, while driving in the direction of Poverty Castle I heard, as I approached the ruined tower a picalo duet.

Gower. — A picalo duet!

Mrs. Smile. — A picalo duet, and who do you suppose was accompanying his lordship ?

Gower. — Who ?

Mrs. Smile. — The organist. Miss Revere. She (*With a smile*) plays the picalo.

Gower. — Learned it, no doubt, to please his lordship.

Mrs. Smile. — Certainly!   And what do you suppose they were playing ; this matter of fact heavy witted, impassive Poverty and the shy, dreamy organist, whom he's given up, Kling's Two Little Finches. (*They laugh.*)

Gower. — Who in the devil is Miss Revere, any-way?

Mrs. Smile. — Nobody knows, but the parson, her guardian ; and who ever heard of his telling anything?

Gower. — She's an American.

Mrs. Smile. — That's true. She came when a child from Colorado to London, where she was educated.

Gower. — Then his lordship hasn't given her up ?

Mrs. Smile. — No, he still toys with her.

Gower. — He'd better be careful. Lady Hamilton will disinherit him.

Mrs. Smile. — She's got to do it before the twentieth, otherwise it won't be in her power.

Gower. — That I've been told, but don't understand.

Mrs. Smile. — One of the conditions of her own in-heritance was this ; to effectually cut Lord Poverty off from the full enjoyments of Heatherstone, its rents and other emoluments, she was to do it, by testimentary de-cree, on or before her sixtieth birth day.

Gower. — I see she becomes sixty on the twentieth. (*Enters* Sirao *from left.*)

Sirao. — *A small dark clean shaven Italian Jew. Nervous, and polite; has a habit, when excited, of drawing his mouth to one side and inhaling the air through his closed teeth, mak-ing an andible sound. Wears a dress suit. Has a dark top coat on, left pocket of which is torn exposing white lining. His shirt front is badly rumpled. Presents unmistakable evidences of having been in a struggle.*) Pardon, madame, I was detained. My son was out of the building with my keys in his pocket.

Mrs. Smile. — Your son Maxey ?

Sirao. — Yes madam. My step-son Maxey. (*Goes to door at left and locks it.*) Her's a bad boy, madam.

Gower. — Has he assaulted you ?

Sirao. — (*Laughs.*)We had a little struggle. (*Approaching painting.*)

Mrs. Smile. — I'm sorry to trouble you, Signior.

Sirao. — Delighted, madam! I drew and locked the

curtains, (*Adjusts reflectors, turns on gas and unlocks clasps of curtains*) when the ladies and gentlemen entered the banqueting hall. The room was packed; all were delighted with the great painting (*Draws curtains*).

Mrs. Smile. — Beautiful!

Gower. — Grand, by Love!

Mrs. Smile. — It's sublime!

Sirao. — (*Looks in direction of left entrance, as though expecting some one.*) " Van Elfins Peace." (*In impressive tones*). The greatest work of this century. The anxious dream of philanthropy, becalmed and materialized. A petition to humanity to forgo the logic of blood and iron, and cleave to the faith of arbitration. (*Enters Taylor at right.*)

Taylor (*A servant*). — Please (*To Gower.*) Sir (*Bowing*) and Madam, the opening. (*Bows and retires, right.*)

Mrs. Smile. — (*To Gower.*) Come! (*To Sirao.*) We will return later, Signior. (*Goes to left, followed by Gower.*) Thank you. (*To Gower.*) Let us enter the ball room from the main hall.

Gower. — It's a grand painting! (*Exeunt Mrs. Smile and Gower.*)

Sirao. — (*Reflects, looks at his shirt front.*) Maxey is a young tiger. (*Puts keys into coat pocket, they fall to the floor.*) He's (*Sees torn coat for first time.*) a devil, a devil! (*Enraged.*) Next time I'll choke him worse, the (*Taking off his coat and laying it on the table.*) damm—devil! Leaves my door open! (*Looks in direction of door to right.*) Takes my keys and leaves the building without my permission. (*Looks about him.*) If any one saw the other Van Elfin, I'd be ruined. (Looks in direction of door.) Leaves my door unlocked, the devil! I must get out of this town! (*Contemplates painting.*) The copy is an improvment on the original. (*Sees Maxey, who appears at left with hat on and small grip sack in his hand.*) He's going to run away. (Maxey *disappears.*) Maxey! Maxey! *Forna indietro ; Forna indietro.* (*Come back! come back!*) *Non hai denaro!* (*You' have no money.*) He's going! (*Alarmed.*) He must'nt—I need him. He must help me get the original back to London! (*Calls.*) *Forna indietro!* (*Come back! To himself.*) I'm a fool to have quarreled with the boy. He may talk. (*Exit left.* Helen Rushfoot *appears at right. Looks cautiously from entrance.*)

Helen (*Pretty blond of eighteen. Low voice*). — I must see Jack tonight (*Enters*). No one here? Just what I thought. As soon as Miss Revere comes she must guard that entrance, (*Looks toward right.*) while I'll work the telephone and keep my eye in this direction. (*Goes to left and looks into hall.*) Oh dear! I wish I had Jack on the other end (*Looks at telephone*) of that wire. Why don't Effie come? Time is precious! I won't wait. (*Rings telephone. The hammer strikes gong violently. She retreats in alarm.*) The spiteful thing! (*Her call is answered.*) They've answered, I'll muffle the bell. (*Puts handkerchief between hammer and gong.*) Oh dear! (*Over phone.*) Give me the Royal George Inn. (*Aside, as she listens.*) Poor Jack! across the road — in a foreign land — among strangers — in the hotel. (*Over phone.*) Is this the Royal George? It is? Please find Mr. Randolph, and ask him to step to the telephone. (*Listens.*) What? (*Listens.*) You'll hold the phone and ring me up. (*Listens.*) Thank you! (*Hangs phone.*) Why don't Effie come. (*Looks about her for a moment, and then advances to mirror. Throws her train out, takes few steps to get effect. Switches train about and steps in opposite direction. During these, and other maneuvers, she continues her lines at convenient intervals.*) She — knows — I'm dying — to see Jack. I've told her — everything — Effie's in love too. She'll admit it some day. (*Reflects.*) I wonder who her lover is? (*Enters Effie Revere.*)

Effie (*Beautiful brunette of eighteen*). — My! I'm afraid.

Helen. — Of what?

Effie. — That you're going to be indiscreet.

Helen. — I'm use to it. It's my strong point, Jack says. I've called the inn up, they're after Jack.

Effie. — My! You have?

Helen. — Yes.

Effie. — Are you sure Helen — ?

Helen (*Interrupting*). — Of what?

Effie. — That you're not doing wrong?

Helen. — I'm only scheming to see my Jack.

Effie. — Yes, but your father.

Helen (*Interrupting*). — He's scheming himself.

Effie. — To accomplish what?

Helen. — To elect brother George to parliament. Giving the English Arbitration taffy, and they're scheming in return working the American cousin racket, (*Seriously.*) to get my dear country into trouble. What's Arbitration or a seat in parliament anyway, compared to Jacks' love? (*Taking letter from her bosom.*) Dear boy! (*Kisses it.*) This is his last letter to me. (*Sorrowfully.*) Written in awful anguish.

Effie. — When did he write it?

Helen. — The day he learned, that I'd been hustled into exile on account of him. Shall I read it?

Effie. — Please do.

Helen (*Reads*). — "My Prize Angel. (*Almost in tears.*) Say, that orthodox, straight-laced, thin haired, she-professor of the Fifth Avenue Ladies Seminary says that you were crowded abroad by your indignant father, on learning of our secret correspondence, and surreptitious meetings. Neither your father, nor that Vassa-tainted old spinster, can break up the combine.

I sail by the next steamer. Your only Jack."

Effie. — The combine! What's that?

Helen. — Our consolidated hearts!

Effie. — How poetic!

Helen. — Is your admirer poetical?

Effie (*Shaking her head*). — No, but he's fond of music, and he's the finest waltzer in Dorchester Oaks.

Helen. — Is he at the hop?

Effie. — Yes.

Helen (*Laughing*). — Now Miss Awfully-afraid and Never-tell beauty, Ill find out who your mash is.

Effie (*Alarmed*). — How?

Helen (*Laughing*). — I'll watch the dancers.

Effie. — He's not going to dance tonight.

Helen. — Oh Effie. That's mean. Why?

Effie. — Because his foot troubles him.

Helen. — Do you love him?

Effie. — I don't dare to. I don't understand him. He's awfully odd. At times I think he hasn't a heart. He hasn't the least sentiment. He's blunt, and matter of fact.

Helen. — Has he proposed?

Effie. — Almost—one day. Oh wasn't I frightend! (*Telephone rings.*)

Helen. — There's Jack!

Effie. — My! Oh dear! But I'll watch.

Helen (*At telephone*). — Yes? (*Listens Expresses her recognition of Jack's voice by apparent agitation.*) Oh, Jack I'm so glad to see you! (*Listens.*) What? Oh Jack I'm dying Jack—(*Listens*) I don't see you? But Jack, I'm dying —(*Listens.*) What? (*Listens.*) Some one may overhear me? (*To Effie.*) I didn't think of that. (*Over phone affecting a masculine voice.*) Say Randolph, the Anglo-American Arbitration League is giving a hop in the building opposite your hotel; come over. (*Listens.*) No ticket? That don't matter. Come over. Unknown in Americans in dress suits are having a soft snap all over England, these days. You have n't a dress suit, your trunk has not arrived? (*Voices heard in reception room.*)

Effie. — Some one coming! Helen! Quick, quick!

Helen. — (*Over phone*). — Jack, Jack! Listen! Get a suit and come to room where picture is on exhibition. (*Listens.*) What—meet you at entrance?

Effie. — Oh, Helen you're mad! Some one is coming!

Helen. — Some one is coming, Jack! Good bye! (*Hangs phone.*)

Effie. — My! (*Hurries to left.*) Come! (*Exit.*)

Helen. — But Jack has n't a dress suit. The campaign has opened! (*Exit.*

Enters Rushfoot *and* Maby *smoking.*)

Rushfoot — (*A tall, slim, wirey man, about fifty five : has dark, piercing, snapping eyes, smooth face, long thick, black, Indian hair, that's cut strait around, and falls just to his coat collar. Has a habit of projecting his lower lip up-*

wards. When excited, he turns his head with such rapidity, that his hair switches about, and at times, into his face, when he throws it back, over his ears, with a quick, jerky motion. In temper, he gesticulates with great fierceness. Is nervously polite, and at times theatrical. Though the features of his face are seldom in repose, he has a kind look and often smiles.)

Just a few puffs in the corridor.

Maby. — Arbitration with the States will be a great thing for England.

Rushfoot. — That's right. Sure, England wants Arbitration. She wants it badly. She needs it in her business.

Maby. — Colonel, why dont you talk seriously?

Rushfoot. — Never was more serious in my life!

Maby. — (*Earnestly.*) Are you, or are you not, in favor of Arbitration?

Rushfoot. — (*Confidentially.*) Well George, away down in the thirteenth level, I'm like the Administration senators, who vote for the bill, praying to God it won't pass. I'm playing Englands game. 'Tis all politics with me. I'm trying to elect you to Parliament. (*Exeunt Rushfoot and Maby left.*)

Helen — (*Peeping around corner of right entrance*). Gone! (*Enters.*) — Now to see Jack! He told me to meet him at the front entrance, and I'll do it. We've agreed to obey each other without a murmur. 'Tis the way to preserve the combine, so Jack says. (*Looks out left entrance.*) Think of it; so near and yet so far! (*Looks at her gown.*) This dress is so conspicuous. (*Looks out again.*) The coast is clear. (*Looks at gown again.*) I wish I had a dark wrap. (*See's Siraos coat, and hat.*) Whose coat is this? I'll put it on. (*Puts coat on, gathers her skirts about her; goes to mirror.*) I'm safe. No one will recognize me. (*Puts hat on.*) I'm off! (*Exit left, affecting man's stride. Enters Taylor from right with an armfull of coats. Throws them on the table*)

Taylor. — Hi siy! These 'ere (*Wiping his face with handkerchief.*) Arbitration gentlemen will have to build a

larger coat room, hif they give many more 'ops. Hue!
hue! (*Wiping his face again.*) Now if the art chap don't
object, I'll turn his quarters hinto a coat room hannex.
I't he does object, I'll get Maxey to give him another bout,
like the one he gave him around the corner a few minutes
ago. Ha, ha, ha, the young Italian is a scratcher! The
old chap don't treat him right. He's pounding hand
abeating hof him all the time. Maxey his a good honest
lad so every one says. Now for a few more bob!
(*Shakes coin in his pocket. Noise in hall, left entrance.
Exit right. Enters* Lord Poverty, Helen *clinging to his arm.
Siraos hat is pulled down on her head. She holds skirts of
overcoat tightly to prevent her dress from falling, causing coat
to bunch out behind in an odd fashion.*)

Helen (*Surpressing her alarm*). — Oh Lord Poverty, (*Rolling her eyes.*) you've saved me from an awful fate!

Poverty. — (*An angular Englishman, about twenty six.
Is cleanly shaven, has dark, strait her, brushed close to his
head, and parted in the middle. Pronounced features, with
absolute immobility of expression. 'Precipitous in speech, with
jerky, strong, ascending intonation from the first word of a
sentence, to nearly its close. When, though his tone becomes
less pronounced, it still rises to a close that's always abrupt.
While apparently cold, he's possessed of a warm heart and
beneath, what appears to be an almost stupid mind, is quick
perception, and good sense.*) Fancy!

Helen (*Confidentially*). — I'm wildly romantic, but keep
quiet about it! (*Removes hat and coat.*)

Poverty. — Quiet—of course! Where were you
going?

Helen. — I longed to catch a glimpse of an alien night
in a foggy town. No, no, no, I'm mixed! I was after a
breath of the exhilerating gloom of—Oh dear! (*Disgusted.*) Lord Poverty! (*In matter of fact manner.*) I was making for the front entrance when fortunately I bumped
against you, otherwise I would have run right into father's
arms. He would have been shocked, shocked. (*Aside.*)
I'll get him to hep Jack with a dress suit.

Poverty. — Tlhat's it.

Helen (*Inquiringly*). — Father was out of the building without his hat. What was he doing?

Poverty. — Buying the States.

Helen. — Buying the States?

Poverty. — Yes. The States, your own States. They 've made a new map about them. He stepped around the corner.

Helen. — Oh yes buying a map of the United States.

Poverty. — That's it.

Helen (*Aside*). — I'll approach the dress suit business gradually and cautiously. (*To* Poverty. *Confidentially.*) Father is going to return to America after the nineteenth, you ought to go with him. Father says you saw but little of the United States when you were there before.

Poverty. — Only a little. Some day I'll take a new look at the States. Of course—why not. But you see I'm waiting.

Helen. — Waiting? (*Aside*) That reminds me so is Effie. I must see her at once. (*To* Poverty.) Oh Lord Poverty pardon me a moment, only a moment, I'll come right back. (*Exit right.*)

Poverty. — (*Reflecting.*) I must try me hand at this girl—of course—to keep the peace. Me aunt wants me to marry her. Miss Rushfoot might engage herself to me for a week or two, until after the twentieth, to fool me aunt. I mustn't lose the money and Heatherstone. Heatherstone is a fine asset. (*Takes letter from his pocket.*) Of course! (*Reads.*) "Helen Rushtoot is eligible. Press your addresses earnestly and delicately. Remember the twentieth is at hand. An engagement at once with the American girl will answer. To inherit Heatherstone, you must marry at least five thousand a year." (*Reflects.*) That's it—to inherit money I must marry cash. No wedding fee, no funeral stuff. Of course- I'll scheme away at the girl—delicately and earnestly—to trick me aunt. (*Helen enters right.*)

Helen. — I'm so glad you didn't go, Lord Poverty. You said you were waiting for something before going to the United States.

Poverty. — Yes, yes! I'm waiting for a little luck, a little grave yard luck.

Helen. — Grave yard luck?

Poverty. — That's it. You see I've an old aunt, who's bothering along with a bit of breath in her, when that leaves her, I'm to have money and Heatherstone, provided I can keep her tricked up to the twentieth of this month.

Helen. — (*Holding her breath with a comical expression of horror.*) Lord Poverty:

Poverty. — (*Without noticing Helen's last exclamation.*) And then I don't mind doing the States.

Helen. — (*With affected indignation.*) Your aunt ought not to leave you a dollar.

Poverty. — Of course the cemetery ticket may prove a blank. If it does I'll jog away to the States anyway— why not?

Helen. — (*Sarcastically.*) In search, no doubt, of some American girl with money.

Poverty. — With money—of course   I'd knock about a little for the money—to be sure.

Helen. — The money! What about the girl?

Poverty. — The girl – yes, yes—of course—the poor thing—I forgot about her, but the inheritance trick suits me best.

Helen. — Lord Poverty, I'm surprised!

Poverty. — Ah – but it's better. The legacy trick is always the best. In that case, you see, the money's yours; but when a girl bribes a chap to marry her, she's forever after picking away at his subsidy, begging a pound for this thing, and a shilling for that.

Helen. — (*Solemnly and searchingly.*) Then the girl you marry, must have money.

Poverty. — That's it—I'm forbidden to bother with anything but cash.

Helen. — And to please Lady Hamilton —

Poverty. — Not to please her—to get her money.

Helen. — Lord Poverty you can never be a friend of mine – (*Sorrowfully and looking downward*) and I wanted you to be so much.

Poverty. — So much—of course.

Helen, — I wanted some one to confide in.

Poverty. — I'll take your confidence—I'll be your friend.

Helen. — Oh you're so kind! (*Approaching Poverty in confidential manner.*) Say. (*Low voice.*) Can a fellow buy a swallow tail in town in ten minutes, right off, just now?

Poverty. — A swallow tail?

Helen. — Yes.

Poverty. — Is that a new American drink?

Helen. — No, no, It's not a drink! It's a suit of clothes, an evening dress suit, such as you have on.

Poverty. — Not under ten days.

Helen. — (*In despair.*) Lord Poverty I'm in trouble. (*Tragically.*) Can you realise the sorrow of a young girls agitated bosom? You must help me.

Poverty. — I may be able to help you to a cocktail— to a swallow-tail—but the agitated bosom—(*Looking at Helen.*) Are you in love?

Helen. — (*Collecting herself, nods assent.*) Yes—but you don't know what it is to be that way. (*Nervously working her foot, and looking at her shoe.*)

Poverty. — Who's the chap?

Helen. — Would you like to meet him?

Poverty. — Why not?

Helen. — (*Looking upwards.*) But he's away—way— off—across—the—wide, wide—(*Looking at Poverty.*) Will you never tell?

Poverty. — Never.

Helen. — While you live and I live, and Jack lives?

Poverty. — While anybody lives.

Helen. — He's away off across the wide, wide street.

Poverty. — At the hotel?

Helen. — No, no he's hanging around in front of this building—, without a dress suit on. He has just arrived from America. He's registered at the inn as Jack Randolph, but his real name is Jack Randolph Robins, jr. Father exiled me (*Sorrowfully*) to prevent me from seeing him, and all because he heard that Jack was wild, but he isn't. (*Putting handkerchief to her eyes.*) Father has condemned him without a trial, without even, ever having seen him. Help us Lord Poverty.

Poverty. — I can't help you.

Helen. — (*Turning her head but with handkerchief still to her eyes.*) Why?

Poverty. — Me own breast is in a bad shape. I'm in love—

Helen. — You in love?

Poverty. — Of course.

Helen. — (*With delight.*) Oh isn't that nice! (*Reflecting.*) But I understand she's got money.

Poverty. — No, she's a poor thing.

Helen. — And you love her in spite of Lady Hamilton.

Poverty. — I'm to trick me aunt.

Helen. — (*Excitedly.*) Do you want help?

Poverty. — I need it.

Helen. — I'll help you.

Poverty. — Who are you going to trick?

Helen. — Nobody—I only want you to help me see Jack every day, and get him a swallow tail to—night. What's your girls name?

Poverty. — Will you never tell?

Helen. — Never!

Poverty. — Until you're dead—while nobody lives? Remember you're a woman.

Helen. — (*Tragically.*) I swear it! What's her name?

Poverty. — Maloney.

Helen. — Maloney, what a funny name! What's her full name?

Poverty. — Effie, Lillian, Maloney, Revere.

Helen.—Not the chapel organist?

Poverty. — Who else?

Helen. — (*Aside.*) Dear Effie. (*To Poverty.*) Why she's an American!

Poverty. — From Colorado.

Helen. — Oh, Lord Poverty—she's the most beautiful girl in Dorchester Oaks. Does she love you?

Poverty. — I think not.

Helen. — And you love her.

Poverty. — Of course, why not?

Helen. — Can't you find out whether or not she loves you?

Poverty. — I'm working away at her.

Helen. — That's the way Jack did to me.

Poverty. — I'll see Jack. (*Reflecting*.) I have seen him.

Helen. — You have?

Poverty. — A bright young chap talked with me at the entrance.

Helen. — (*Delighted*.) That was Jack. What did he say?

Poverty. — He asked me what was going on inside. I told him.

Helen. — And then?

Poverty. — He said he'd have to take the show in that he was a correspondent and art critic of the—some Earth.

Helen. — Glorious, glorious. (*Laughs to herself*.) But what a whopper! (*Aside*.)

Poverty. — The art critic business will keep him knocking about you until the nineteenth.

Helen. — Oh I'm so happy! See Jack right away!

Poverty. — Give me a line to him.

Helen. — Pronounce the word " Combine " and Jack will be at your feet. See him right away.

Poverty. — But about me own breast troubles—you must help me. You see if I'm engaged to money before the twentieth Heatherstone is mine.

Helen. — How can I help you?

Poverty. — You know Benson?

Helen. — Lady Hamilton's maid?

Poverty. — That's the thing. She's a spy, she's watching us.

Helen. — Watching us?

Poverty. — That's it. She's a bad old hag about the affair.

Helen. — What affair, and why is she watching me?

Poverty. — I've told Lady Hamilton that you were mushed—(*Helen though horrified laughs.*) Isn't it mushed you Americans say?

Helen. — No, mashed—and you've told your aunt that I was mashed on you?

Poverty. — That's it. You see Lady Hamilton wants me to take you over.

Helen. — Take me over?

Poverty. — Of course. On the altar, money and all, marry you.

Helen. — Well you can't. No person living can take me—What do you call it?

Poverty. — Up—on the Altar.

Helen. — Up, over or down on the altar, but Jack Randolph Robins jr, of New York City.

Poverty. — Me aunt don't know that. If she thinks I've got a show for your money, she'll not disinherit me.

Helen. — Oh, Lord Poverty the idea of saying that I was mashed on you. (*Aside.*) He's got more cheek than Jack.

Poverty. — You see I'm after Heatherstone. It's a fine asset.

Helen. — So you are scheming?

Poverty. — That's it—for Maloney money and Heatherstone. Can't you try me until the twentieth? Agree to marry me, as a joke.

Helen. — Oh Lord Poverty, I couldn't! (*Laughs.*)

Poverty. — Ah, but you must.

Helen. — (*Laughs.*) The idea!

Poverty. — Have me. Of course—why not?

Helen. — I'll think about it. (*Laughs.*)

Poverty. — Whenever Benson is about, be mushed-mashed on me. You see, between Lady Hamilton and Benson, they're trying to force Maloney away from me.

Helen. — Does Effie know it?

Poverty. — No.

Helen. — Poor girl. Lord Poverty please see Jack right away.

Poverty. — Right away! (*Going toward left.*)

Helen. — Don't forget the swallow tail.

Poverty. — And remember our engagement.

Helen. — Will you do everything to help Jack and me?

Poverty. — Why not?

Helen. — Then it's a bargain! (*Laughs.*) Is n't it funny. But you must n't tell Jack. He's awfully jealous at times. (Rushfoots *voice heard in hall at left.* Poverty *looks out.*)

Poverty. — The Colonel!

Helen. — Who's with him?

Poverty. — Jack—of the Earth.

Helen. — (*Alarmed*). Jack?

Poverty. — Yes, the critic.

Helen. — (*Hurrying to right followed by Poverty.*) Jack and father together!

Poverty. — That's it. (*Exeunt* Helen *and* Poverty right. *Enter* Rushfoot *and* Jack *left.*)

Jack. — (*A handsome young man about twenty one. Demonstratively.*) As I was saying, as an American you see my awful position. I'm here with positive instructions to write up the hop (*Looking at the painting.*) and to size up the—artistic—merits of—this—(*Hesitates and points.*) thing here. The artistic business I can do to morrow. But the hop Sir I must be present at the hop · on the floor—a part of it—a joyous fragment of the gliding throng.

Rushfoot. — (*Reflecting.*) And you can't get a dress suit?

Jack. — No where.

Rushfoot. — And they won't let you on the floor without one?

Jack. — Not a foot! Think of it! Because my vest isn't cut that way, (*Turning his vest low and exposing his shirt front.*) and my coat this, (*Turning the skirt of his coat in.*) I'm stood off—prevented from doing my duty—my bread and butter jeopardized (*Looks at Rushfoot.*) What size coat do you wear, Mr.—? Let me see, what is your name?

Rushfoot. — (*Half indignant yet smiling.*) Rushfoot—Colonel Rushfoot.

Jack. — (*Alarmed and aside.*) Great Scott! But I'll not weaken. (*To Rushfoot.*) Say Colonel, in this emergency, when my bread is imperilled, my butter threatened, couldn't you? (*Aroused by the idea.*) Hold on Colonel! Not a word—I've got an idea. My vest must be turned down so, (*Illustrating.*) My coat cut off so. (*Illustrating.*) Hurrah! I'll thwart the designs against the only things I love—my bread and butter. Say Colonel, have you a knife or a pair of shears in your pocket?

Rushfoot. — No, I don't happen to have even the shears. (*Laughs.*)

Jack. — (*Discovers shears on table.*) Here's a pair. Good! (*Takes off his coat puts it on table, cuts front of skirts off. Pins part of vest down exposing skirt front. Takes off necktie, examines it, find it won't do. Pulls out white lining that answers purpose. Turns swivelled mirror around concealing all but his head, and dresses. Continuing his lines during process of cutting coat and dressing.*) You're an American?

Rushfoot. — Yes.

Jack. — That's great! I knew you were. (*Looking at Rushfoot.*) Hallo! You're Rushfoot the great mine owner, Colonel Rushfoot of Colorado. You own the Slopper of Cripple Creek.

Rushfoot. — One of the owners.

Jack. — Why do you call it the Slopper?

Rushfoot. — (*Aside*) This young man is too fresh. (*To Jack.*) It's so full of gold, that every time it's struck with a pick the bullion slops over, and falls into the dividend buckets.

Jack. — (*Aside.*) He's guying me. (*To Rushfoot.*) Say Colonel I own a few shares of Slopper Extension.

Rushfoot. — Keep them—keep them—my boy! We're

liable to strike it rich on the Extension any day. (*Aside.*)
That's all that's safe to say to a newspaper man. I must
change the subject. (*To Jack.*) A desperate expedient,
(*Laughing.*) sacrificing that fine coat.

Jack. — That's no sacrifice for a representative of the
Katonah Earth. What's a coat tail to a mans conscience?

Rushfoot. — The management of the Earth don't expect
you to sacrifice the latter.

Jack. — N—o—of—course not—certainly not, not
the Katonah Earth.

Rushfoot. — The Earth has a great circulation I pre-
sume.

Jack. — Three thousand tons a day.

Rushfoot. — Tons! Oh yes, Ha, ha, ha, modern jour-
nalism. Your press consumes three thousand tons of
paper daily.

Jack. — Every day.

Rushfoot. — Good circulation, then ?

Jack. — Suffers awfully at times.

Rushfoot. — With what?

Jack. — Junk-shop congestion. Say Colonel, if I had
a pair of white gloves!!

Rushfoot. — (*Handing Jack his own.*) You can have
mine, my modest friend. (*Smiles.*)

Jack. — (*Taking gloves.*) Thanks. Now for a buttonnaire. A hundred Sloppers for a buttonnaire. Colonel,
Colonel!

Rushfoot. — Well.

Jack. — Can you spare one of those buds of yours,
and just a little of that maiden hair.

Rushfoot. — (*Taking a large white chrysanthemum from
vase on mantel.*) Here's what you need. (*Hands it to
Jack.*) 'Twill temper—(*Aside.*) the effulgent glare of your
expansive cheek.

Jack. — (*Stepping from behind mirror neatly and attrac-
tively dressed.*) Yours—truly—Jack—Randolph. Are you
engaged for the next waltz? (*Bowing to an imaginary
lady.*)

Ruhsfoot. — (*Astonished.*) The transformation is marvellous. My boy, you're a genius! On my honor—a genius.

Jack. — Colonel, can't you introduce me to a handsome young lady?

Rushfoot. — Sure. A young man who meets emergencies in this manner, deserves to know the fairest.

Jack. — Thank you Colonel, thank you just present me to—

Rushfoot. — Either an English or American girl!

Jack. — (*Reflecting.*) A—h—English. No, no, an American—I'll be selfish and take the best.

Rushfoot. — I'll introduce you to my daughter. (*Enter Helen and Effie.*)

Jack. — (*Aside.*) My prize Angel!

Rushfoot. — (*To Helen.*) Helen?

Helen. — (*Hastens to her fathers side. Takes his arm and looks into his face tenderly and coyly, though excited.*) Brother George wants to see you right away.

Rushfoot. — What's up?

Helen. — The Prince of Wales is to be present at the celebration.

Rushfoot. — Good! Wales is a trump! (*Turning to Jack.*) A great item for the Earth. (*Jack bows.*)

Helen. — And he's to spend the night at Devon House!

Rushfoot. — (*To Jack.*) Hear that my boy? We're to put Wales up over night, and to feed him. Another item. (*Aside.*) This fact assures my—son—in - law's election. (*To Jack.*) By George you shall meet the Prince. I'll introduce you to—(*Looks at Helen.*) That reminds me —Mr. Randolph I present you to my daughter, and to Miss Revere. Helen, make it pleasant for this young gentleman, he's an American. (Helen *bows with great reserve.* Effie *bows and turn aside to conceal her smiles.* Jack *bows.*)

Helen. — I shall try. (*To Jack.*) An American? (*Aside.*) Isn't he handsome!

Jack. — (*Bowing.*) From New York. (*Aside.*) Isn't she a stunner.

Rushfoot. — (*Going to right entrance.*) I must find George.

The Prince is a brick! That's right! (*Exit* Rushfoot. *Effie crosses to left. Helen and Jack look at each other a moment, and then rush into each others arms.*)

Jack. — Helen!

Helen. — Jack! Oh Jack I'm so glad to see you!

Jack. — (*Kissing Helen.*) Words! words! they're not in it. Actions speak. (*Kisses her again.*) Kisses talk!

Helen. — (*With a gesture and look of warning.*) We must be cautious. (*Jack looks and sees Effie, whose presence he has overlooked.*)

Jack. — Yes we'll defer the kissing.

Helen. — To a more opportune time. Oh Jack—I'm so—

Jack. — Restrain yourself Helen for the good of the combine. (*A lively waltz is now plainly heard from behind scene.*) We can waltz.

Helen. — Yes the combine can waltz—(*Spitefully.*) in the face of the whole world.

Jack. — (*Rolls table to right. Helen hurries to Effie.*) You bet!

Helen. — (*To Effie.*) Get Lord Poverty, and we'll have a little hop all to ourselves. He's the finest waltzer in Dorchester Oaks. (*Laughs.*) And he's fond of music.

Effie. — (*Startled.*) Who told you?

Helen. — I know everything.

Effie. — His foot troubles him.

Helen. — Find him Effie, find him.

Effie. — But his fool.

Helen. — (*Jack and Helen waltz for a moment,*) Oh Jack isn't it glorious. Where did you get your swallow—

Effie. — (*Interrupting.*) Let's all look for his lordship.

Helen. — (*To Jack.*) Yes, Let's find Lord—(*Exeunt right all. Enters Sirao at left.*)

Sirao. — (*Excited.*) Where's my coat? (*Takes hat and coat.*) Maxey is in front of the inn. He must not leave me. I'm afraid of him. He might—yes—I'm afraid of him—I was a fool to choke him. (*Turns gas of reflectors low darkening the stage.*) I should have waited until I got to Italy. The young devil! Yes I must coax him back.

(*Exit* Sirao *left passing* Poverty *who enters with bundle, throws same on table. Stands for a moment and listens to the waltz. Takes off his overcoat, in so doing, the right sleave catches in cuff link of skirt. He pulls the sleave inside out to the elbow grasps the other sleave in his left hand, and holds it out as though it were the extended arm of a waltzing partner. The inside of the overcoat, which is exposed is lined with light colored material, except collar, which is of darker shade. In attempting to remove his overcoat in the first instance a white handkerchief drops to the floor, this he holds in his mouth and waltzes. In the subdued light he appea to dance with a phantom figure. The conformation of the lining of his overcoat suggest the form of a woman. Enter Helen, Effie and Jack.*)

Helen. — Where can he be? Some one has turned down the light. (*Discovers* Poverty.) Here's his lordship.

Effie. — (*Aside.*) Who's the lady? (*Helen turns up lights.*)

Jack. — One more whirl.

Helen. — (*To* Poverty.) Where have you been?

Poverty. — (*Who has ceased to waltz is now seen in dress suit much to large for him. To* Helen. *Pointing to bundle on table.*) Hustling for Jack. Why not? (Helen *laughs.*) I missed the critic, but I got him a cocktail, a swallow tail.

Helen — (*Introducing* Poverty *and* Jack.) Mr. Randolph. Lord Poverty. (Jack *bows.*)

Poverty. — (*To* Jack.) Of course ; Of the Earth.

Jack. — (*To* Helen.) The combine is waisting time. One more whirl.

Poverty. — That's it. (*Helen and Jack waltz. In waltzing past left entrance, the formers discovers* Benson, *who appears at entrance in position, that commands view only of part of stage.*)

Helen. — (*To* Poverty.) Benson! Benson!

Poverty. — Change partners! (*Change is made without a break in the whirl. When out of* Benson's *view, they exchange partners again, &c., &c.*)

Effie. — (*To* Helen.) Helen let us go.

Helen. — (Helen *beckons to* Jack *and* Effie.) Scoot Jack! scoot! (*Exit* Effie *right, followed by* Jack *who stands*

for moment unobserved by Helen, who with Poverty and for
Bensons *benefit waltzes close to left.*) I'm charmed with Eng-
land.   I never want to leave it.
Poverty. — (*Kissing* Helen.) You never shall. (*Waltz*
ceases music stops.)
Jack — This is fine! (*Enters* Benson, Jack *retires*
excited.)
Benson. — (*A tall spinster about fifty, bows.*) Your
lordship. (*Hands Poverty a letter – Poverty takes letter with-*
out noticing Benson—The latter retires.)
Poverty. —(*Opening letter and looking after Benson.*) She's
getting thin. I've killed her Tom.
Helen. — Her Tom?
Poverty. — Yes—cat. A moment, from me aunt.
(*Reads.*) "At dusk last Wednesday evening a picalo duet
was heard on terrace of Poverty castle. Who was your
musical companion?" (*Reflects.*) Do you play the picalo?
Helen. — (*Surprised.*) I never saw one!
Poverty. — (*Aside.*) Then me best asset is gone.
Helen. — Come Lord Poverty. Jack is waiting.
Poverty. — (*Following* Helen *to right.*) Of course.
(*Exeunt. Enter Mrs. Smile and Gower left.*)
Mrs. Smile. — (*Excited.*) An unusual commotion among
the Mabys! What does it mean? What new surprise has
Mrs. Rushfoot—Hyphen Maby in store for us?
Gower. — Rushfoot Hyphen Maby—Ha, ha, ha! Hy-
phen!
Mrs. Smile. — Yes. A Yankee device. The escut-
cheon of the social struggler. But why the excitement?
Gower. — The Prince of Wales is to be present at the
celebration.
Mrs. Smile. — (*Coldly.*) That means Mabys election.
Gower. — Quite so. And his Highness with three
members of the royal household is to honor Mrs. Rushfoot Hyphen Maby by a visit to Devon House, where he
remains until the afternoon of the twentieth.
Mrs. Smile. — (*Aside, with conflicting emotions.*) Damn
the Prince of Wales! (*To Gower.*) This means.
Gower. — (*Interrupting.*) My lady Maby.

Mrs. Smile.— (*Laughing bitterly.*) If we were only Yankees! My lady Maby! (*Collecting herself.*) My wrap please. 'Tis on the chair near the orange plants. I must go.

Gower. — Are you ill?

Mrs. Smile. — Only chilly. (*Exit* Gower—*right.*) My lady Maby—entertaining royalty. Its too bad, that Emma has lost her nasel twang. Her " shants " and " cants " would intensify the shop-made grandeur of Devon halls. (*Enters* Sirao *followed by* Maxey. Mrs. Smile *stands behind mirror.*)

Sirao. — Come Maxey, let us be friends.

Maxey. — Parli italiano. (*Speak Italian.*)

Sirao. — Speak Italian? No Maxey you understand English. You must learn to talk it.

Maxey. — Voglio il mio istrumento. (*I want my model.*)

Sirao. — You want your model. Then you're going.

Maxey. — (*Pointing to side door.*) Voglio il mio instrumento. (*I want my model.*)

Sirao. — You want your model? (*Unlocks door and takes small picture frame with painting from room.*) Your silly device for framing pictures! You think because you can throw the end of a frame back like that. (*Illustrating by throwing back the end of a frame, that swings backwards allowing painting to be drawn out at end with ease.*) And pull a painting out like that—(*Illustrating.*)

Maxey. — (*Pointing to large painting.*) Quale inutile strumento adopera! (*The silly device you use.*)

Sirao. — I use your silly device. Yes to please you, you going devil! So you're going to leave your father?

Maxey. — Lei non è mio! padre. (*You're not my father!*)

Sirao. — Not your father! (*Angrily.*) No thank God, you—take your model and get out of here. (*Throws it violently on floor. Maxey takes it up, and in a violent rage, attempts to drive it through canvas of large painting.*)

Maxey. — Canaglia, guastero il suoginoco. (*I'll spoil your game, you fiend.*)

Sirao. — *Rushes between painting and* Maxey.) You'll

spoil my game? (*Conciliatory.*) Don't call me a fiend
Maxey. You would'nt destroy the great painting, would
you ?

Maxey. — (*Hurries to left.*) The Van Elfin (*Pointing.*)
is no gooda—copy-copy—I'll talka English I'll talka English to alla manna in towna (*Pointing to painting.*) A copy
—a copy. (*Exit* Maxey.)

Sirao. — (*Following Maxey.*) I'll kill the devil! (*Exit*)

Mrs. Smile. — (*Stepping from behind mirror excited.*)
What does all this mean ? Only a copy! Did anyone
hear ? (*Goes to left. Looks into hall.*) No one! The secret
is mine alone. (*Enters Gower with wrap.*)

Gower. — Yes tis getting chilly. (*Helps* Mrs. Smile
on with wrap.)

Mrs. Smile. — Yes.

Gower. — (*Looking at painting.*) The Van Elfin is
grand !

Mrs. Smile. — Sublime ! (*Laughing long and loud.*)

Gower. - What are you laughing at ?

Mrs. Smile. — The nonsense of my hostility to poor
Emma Maby. Poor Emma! (*Continues to laugh.*)

— END OF FIRST ACT —

THE SECOND ACT.

One week has-clapsed between the First and second Acts.

The Scene is the entrance to outer court yard of Poverty castle. *To the left is an old building, with arched entrance from road in the centre, terminating in a ruined tower in left back-ground. To the right, amid a growth of evergreen stands a smaller tower, which like the former is roofless and without windows. Connecting these towers in broken outlines is an ancient parapet, elevated slightly from the stage. Again to the right, overhanging the driveway which continues from arched entrance, it is supposed, to inner castle yard, are giant trees with leafless and fantastic branches. Farther in the background to the right is a path, leading, it's supposed, through neglected shrubbery to ruined tower. To the right of arched entrance are stone steps leading to entrance of old building. On each side of entrance is a nitch, in one stands statue of knight in armor, the other is empty. The building walls, trees and shrubbery suggest neglect and decay. The outlook from the parapet is upon a beautiful country, of woodland and meadows; the whole. Scene being animated by the glow of a rare December sunset. As the curtain rises* Poverty *and* Effie *are discovered seated at an old stone table, in the background, upon which are bottles, glasses fruit, &c.* Jack *and* Helen *stand near arched entrance,* Helen *is eating an apple and holding in her hand a large serviette.* Jack *holds a glass half filled with wine.* He *is attempting to engage* Helen *in a serious conversation; but the latter is too full of merriment to be otherwise than indifferent to his mood.*

Jack. — Do you know, I havn't seen you alone one moment, since the night of the hop?

Helen. — Do I know it, of course I do.

Jack. — (*Seriously.*) During the cheerless, black, gloomy, and wretched days, hours and minutes that have intervened between that night and this second, have you had one thought of anything or any person on the earth or in the waters under the earth but of me and the combine.

Helen. — (*Playfully.*) Take a bite.

Jack. - (*Aside.*) She dont know that I saw Poverty kiss her. (*To Helen.*) Helen you dont want to cut the Gordian knot that ties the palpitating cables of our entangled souls do you?

Helen. — Oh Jack, shut up! (*Kisses him with mouthful of apple.*)

Jack. — (*In better spirits.*) You do really love.

Helen. — (*Interrupting.*) I forgot to tell you, Sirao and Maxey have cleared out. The old " dago," got mad because the painting was removed to Devon House without his knowledge. Sister is going to ask you, (*In merry mocking tone.*) the art critic of the Katonah Earth, to hang the great master piece in the new headquarters of the league. (*Earnestly.*) Be ready to meet the new emergency Jack.

Jack. — (*Aside. Showing his cuffs upon which are written notes on art.*) I'm ready to talk a little art. I've recorded the points.

Effie. — (*Calling.*) Helen, Helen! (*The latter joins* Effie *and* Poverty. *An animated conversation follows.* Poverty *points to right.*)

Jack. — (*Aside.*) Poverty kissed her and she didn't object. (*Shaking his head.*) I'll keep my mouth closed and watch.

Helen. — (*To Poverty.*) Where is Bullock?

Poverty. — Keeping his eye on Mrs. Maby and Smile.

Helen. — They mustn't surprise us.

Poverty. — They wont have a chance. They're in the inner court. Bullock will signal us.

Helen. — Won't Sister hear the signal?

Poverty. — She'll think it's a cuckoo.

Effie. — Then Lord Poverty you must keep your promise.

Helen. — Yes, and make a speech. (*Laughs.*)

Jack. — (*Joining party at table.*) Yes, a speech, a speech! from Lord Poverty.

All. — Speech, speech! (*Applause and laughter.*)

Poverty. — (*Standing and holding glass.*) Ladies and —Jack. Let's drink to our candidate. Here's that the votes of today will send Maby to the commons—to get arbitration with the States.

Helen. — (*Interrupting.*) In spite of the fox hunt.

Poverty. — (*Looking at* Helen.) That's it. In spite of the hunt. The Yankee and the Britisher are cousins, they've been—handed down—in natural order from the —same great—great—grand-mothers. (*Cheers and laughter.*) They've the same tongue, why not! But they wag it at each other too much. They must arbitrate and not fight. What's the use of relations yelling-shooting and jabbing away at each other—'Tis awkward. Fancy! I'm through. (*The ladies cheer.*)

Effie. — Now Mr. Randolph 'tis your turn. (*Cheers.*)

Jack. — (*Rising.*) My lord and ladies.

Helen. — Remember Jack, the ears of your countrymen are open.

Jack. — (*Seriously.*) Even in the glow of this generous December sun set, though wine and lemonade floweth, I must be serious. When England disfranchises her rank old squire, the drawling chump that disgraces her gentry, her hereditary shop man, the jockey, and press idiot; when my country-men shall have to reckon with a government that represents only Englands common people, her enlightened middle class and her ancient nobility, will

arbitration have the slightest show? (*With dignity to 'Poverty.*) My lord purge your electorate of these afflicted
classes, and our jingo senators will vote for·an appropria-
tion to fill up the Atlantic, so that John Bull can chuck
his custom dues across the line for all eternity. (*Bellowing
of hounds heard.*)

Helen. — Hark! (*All listen.*) The hounds! (*Hurrying to the parapet.*)

Jack. — (*From parapet.*) I see them! (*Points.*) There,
they're making for the oak grove!

Effie. — I see them! What a grand sight! (*Noise of
clattering hoofs without.*)

Poverty. — Here comes a messenger. (*Bullock in grooms
outfit enters at right on drive way and retires at arched
entrance.*)

Helen. — Another election bulletin I hope.

Poverty. — An election bulletin, that's it. (*Advancing
toward Arched entrance.*) Helen. (*Following Poverty.*) Dear!
I hope brother George will win. He came within seventy votes of being elected last time.

Jack. — (*Who has joined* Poverty *and* Helen.) Only a
majority of seventy to overcome?

Poverty. — The borough has always been close; the
slightest thing may upset either candidate. (*Enters* Bullock.)

Bullock. — (*Hands bulletin to Poverty who hands it to*
Jack.) Hif you please me lud. (*Bullock retires to left.*)

Jack. — (*Reads.*) "A full vote is being cast throughout
most of the district. The contest is a determined one. It
is admitted by all that the election turns on the vote of
Chapel Parish. Forty seven liberal electors were at the
meet this morning. The hunt is the largest of the season.
Maby's friends regard the situation with alarm."

Helen. — "Darn" the hunt!

Jack. — Who got it up?

Helen. — Mrs. Smiles brother. The stupid thing, to
get up a hunt today. (*Noise of clattering hoofs on the road
without.*)

Helen. — Who is it?

Effie. — (*Looking from tower that commands view of road.*)
Helen — your father.

Helen. — (*To* Jack.) Run Jack, run!

Jack. — (*Pointing to open door of old building.*) This
way!

Poverty. — Yes in the armory chambers. (*Exeunt*
Helen, Effie *and* Jack.) The colonel is every where.
(*Enters* Rushfoot, *carrying an ulster, with capacious pocket,
on his arm.*)

Rushfoot. — Bruce can you locate the run?

Poverty. — (*Startled for a moment at the name of Bruce.*)
Yes. (*Going to parapet followed by* Rushfoot.) The leaders
are just emerging from the grove. (*Points—Noise of
hounds again heard.*)

Rushfoot. — I see them. Whose horse is that at the
entrance?

Poverty. — Mine.

Rushfoot. — What? Fleeting John?

Poverty. — Yes.

Rushfoot. — I want him! I'll leave you mine.

Poverty. — Take him.

Rushfoot. — (*To* Bullock *who appears at arched entrance.*)
Tighten John's saddle girt! Quick! (Bullock *retires.*)
I'll break up that hunt if the belly band don't " bust."
Sure! Once a cowboy! always a cow boy!

Poverty. — What are you going to do?

Rushfoot. — Swing from the saddle and bag their
game. (*Pointing to pocket of ulster.*) Sure! (*Unbutton-
ing his suspenders, pulls them from beneath his waistcoat, and
ties them around his waist.*) That's right, Bruce my boy.
(*Detects* Poverty *looking about him.*) Pardon me Poverty,
I know you by that name in Colorado; what a youngster
you were! You havn't forgotten Salida have you?
(*Laughs.*) By the way, what ever became of your partner's little sister? They told me the day he died, that
she was an orphan, that he left her pennyless. (Bullock
*enters at arched entrance, crosses to right retires on road
way.*)

Poverty. — He left nothing. Don't mention Salida.

Rushfoot. — I've respected your wishes for years my
boy; never have —called —you —Bruce—slip of the tongue.
(*Hastens to arched entrance.*) I'll get the recreant liberals
to the polls if the belly band—(*Exit* Rushfoot. *A moment after he his heard to cry " Now John." The rattling
of hoofs follow. Enter* Helen, Effie *and* Jack.)

Helen. — (*Goes to arched entrance followed by* Jack.) He's
gone! (Cuckoo *heard at right.*) Hark! (Cuckoo *heard
again.*) Sister and Smile! (*To* Jack.) Make for the road
Jack.

Jack. — Yes but I'll return to write up Poverty Castle,
you know.

Poyerty. — That's it! (*Exit* Jack, *left arched entrance.*)

Helen. — (*To* Effie.) We'll retreat in this direction.
Get your hat, quick (Helen *and* Effie *put their hats on
and retire to left on path leading to ruined tower.*)

Poverty. — I've told Smile that I'm engaged. She's to
tell no one, but me aunt. (*Exit* Poverty *to join* Helen *and*
Effie. *Enters* Mrs. Smile *from right.*)

Mrs. Smile. — (*Looking back.*) Forever pursuing her
social correspondence! (*Looks about her detects bottles, &c.,
on table.*) Poverty has been entertaining some of his
cronies no doubt. (*Reflects.*) What a sensation —in store
for all England. This will be the story—" To humor
a Yankee wife, who longed to breath the air of a higher
social altitude, an Englishman pays ten thousand pounds
for a piece of counterfeit art; and to seek royal favor,
presents his vulgar purchase to a society of sentimentalists,
suffering from yankeesmite. His Royal Highness, the
Prince of Wales, is asked to honor the occasion by making the presentation speech." It's nauseating—(*Laughs.*)
The explosion that will follow, will rouse such a whirl-
wind of indignation throughout England, that the Maby's
will be blown into the very crevices of social obscurity.
They must n't know the truth until after the mischief is
done. (*Enters* Mrs. Maby *with letters in her hand.*)

You'll rejoice no doubt Emma when the celebration is over, I trust nothing will happen.

Mrs. Maby. — (*A refined handsome and spirited woman about twenty eight.*) It would kill me!

Mrs. Smile. — You are awfully sensitive, I know.

Mrs. Maby. — So far we've been fortunate—except one thing; Signior Sirao left yesterday for Italy. How unfortunate!

Mrs. Smile. — (*Aside.*) Sirao gone! (*To* Mrs. Maby.) Who's to hang the painting?

Mrs. Maby. — I thought of asking Mr. Randolph, to direct the hanging.

Mrs. Smile. — The art critic?

Mrs. Maby. — Yes. (*Enters* Jack *with note book in hand.*) Good evening Mr. Randolph! I was about saying, that we venture to hope for a suggestion from you, when we hang our painting at the league headquarters.

Jack. — Command me, madame.

Mrs. Smile. — (*To* Mrs. Maby.) Isn't it very nice of Mr. Randolpf. (*Enter* Helen *and* Effie.)

Helen. — (*To* Effie.) I'm awfully nervous.

Mrs. Maby. — Rely upon it Mr, Randolph, (*Laughing.*) we shall press your talents into service. (Jack *bows.*)

Helen. — (*To* Effie.) Isn't he graceful, and how handsome! I wish Jack had assumed some other role—I'm afraid—

Jack. — (*To* Mrs. Maby.) You admire the sublimities of the canvas, madame.

Mrs. Maby. — Yes—yet I fear, that one like yourself, skilled in the beauties and subtile refinements of high art, will marvel, when I confess, that though passionately fond of the masters, I can't tell why. (Helen *turns aside to suppress a smile.*)

Jack. — The masters painted up—(*Looking at his cuff.*) painted up—

Helen. — (*Alarmed.*) Any other role! (*To herself.*)

Jack. — Not only to meet the severe exactions of the connoisseur, but (*Looking at cuff.*) down again to ac-

commodate the artistic incapacities of a lady like—yourself.
I mean—

Mrs. Maby. — (*Laughing.*) Like me. But how I
admire Waggmann!

Helen. -- (*To* Effie.) That was great, but awfully im-
pudent. My! (*Puts her hands to her mouth to stifle her merriment.*)

Jack. — (*Affects a dreamy faraway look now and then,
looking at his cuff.*) Waggmann, Waggmann! Look upon
a Waggmann the canvas, vanishes, we behold instead
but an opening—in the mighty gate that swings, that
swings—yes that swings—(*Looking at his cuff.*)—swings
in the portals of the past. Through the forbidden entrance, the living catch glimpses of men—and—women—
(*Hesitates.*)—things and various affairs, that the hand of
Waggmann has rescued from the shades of the forgotten.
(*Looks at cuff—Solemmnly.*) The works of the masters
are but living fragments of the dead past.

Mrs. Maby. — Beautiful!

Mrs. Smile. — Grand!

Helen. — (*Astonished.*) Who told Jack that? (*Aside.*)

Poverty. — (*Who is now seen on the parapet looking
toward the left.*) The run leads—(*To* Mrs. Maby.) Ah
Mrs. Maby, the run leads within a minutes walk of the
Parish.

Mrs. Maby. — (*Joining* Poverty.) Do you see the
hounds?

Poverty. — Yes. (*Pointing.*) The leaders are making
in the direction of Giant Oak. (Poverty *and* Mrs. Maby
disappear to left.)

Mrs. Smile. — (*To* Helen.) Miss Rushfoot did—you—
see much of Lord Poverty when he was in the States?

Helen. — No, never saw him.

Mrs. Smile. — Strange! Your father did.

Helen. — Strange!—Hardly, considering the fact that
at the time, Lord Poverty was in Colorado and I in New
York.

Mrs. Smile. — Let me see Colorado is in North America is it not?

Helen. — (*Looks at* Jack *and smiles.*) Yes, it's been there for some years.

Mrs. Smile. — (*Aside.*) That's a stupid remark. (*To* Helen) Though not fond of new countries, I've often thought—to see Niagara Falls.

Helen. — Ah indeed!

Mrs. Smile. — I suppose you see the Falls as you enter the harbor, or at least before your dock.

Helen. — Yes from Bloomingdale.

Mrs. Smile. — (*Inquiringly.*) I might be fortunate enough to catch a returning steamer on the same day?

Helen. — Very likely.

Mrs. Smile. — Do you like England?

Helen. — No.

Mrs. Smile. — You don't?

Helen. — It's too old—and your fog is so ancient. Your buildings reek with nasty soot. Your churches and monuments with ancient and historic filth. I'm not fond of old islands.

Mrs. Smile. — (*Laughing in a patronizing manner.*) Come my dear, you were certainly charmed with London.

Helen. — I saw but little of it.

Mrs. Smile. — You saw the Tower?

Helen. — The tower, the tower, the Eifle Tower?

Mrs. Smile. — (*Impatiently.*) No—no! The London Tower!

Helen. — Is that in England?

Mrs. Smile. — Where else could it be. (*Aside.*) How stupid! (*To* Helen.) What did you think of Westminster?

Helen. — (*Reflecting.*) Westminster, Westminster?

Mrs. Smile. — Yes the Abbey?

Helen. — Ah yes, that big church that stands on the banks of -(*Hesitates. To* Jack.) Do you know that I can never think of the name of that muddy river that flows through London?

Mrs. Smile. — (*Annoyed.*) The Thames—the Thames.

Helen. — Oh yes. (*To* Mrs. Smile.) Thank you.

Mrs. Smile. — Haven't you studied geography Miss Rushfoot?

Helen. — I was always at the head of my class in geography. I knew every mountain, river, stream, cape, inlet and island in both North and South America?

Mrs. Smile. — But English geography.

Helen. — (*To* Jack.) Do we study English geography in America?

Jack. — (*Who has been writing on table.*) Yes—dont you remember—England comes in among the islands?

Helen. — Ah yes, so it does! Iceland, Madigascar, Ireland.

Jack. — (*Interrupting.*) Long Island.

Helen. — And then England.

Jack. — No, no, Staten Island comes next.

Helen. — Oh yes. Staten Island —Fire—Island.

Jack. — Coney Island.

Helen. — And then England—That's it.

Mrs. Smile. — (*Aside.*) Such ignorance!

Mrs. Maby. — (*Who now appears —advances to middle of stage followed by* Poverty.) Come Lizzie—let us walk in the direction of the Parish. (Mrs. Maby *goes toward arched entrance followed by* Mrs. Smile. *and* Poverty - *The latter speaks to Effie as he passes—-Effie nods assent and gets her wrap.*) We may get the last returns. (*Exeunt* Mrs. Maby, Mrs. Smile *and* Poverty.)

Jack. — (*Going toward door of old building to left.*) I'll keep my eye on Smile and your sister from the back windows. (*Exit* Jack.)

Effie. — (*To* Helen.) His Lordship insists on my putting on my wrap.

Helen. — Isn't he kind to you!

Effie. — Yes. He's like a brother.

Helen. — Do you think it's nice to have a brother? I don't mean a real brother—one that tells you to shut up, and things like that, but a brother that isn't a brother— the kind that falls in love with you.

Effie. — I'm not sure that I do.

Helen. — Jack commenced with me that way.

Effie. — He did?

Helen. — Yes—but the brother business didn't last three days. Your's has lasted longer, hasn't it?

Effie. — (*Laughing.*) Yes—five months.

Helen. — That's too long. Why! I would have died if Jack had kept up that nonsense a day longer.

Effie. — You're in love. (*Looking at* Helen.)

Helen. — And so are—

Effie. — No.

Helen. — You ought to be, it's so nice.

Effie. — (*Laughing.*) I never expect to be.

Helen. — (*Sorrowfully.*) Poor girl.

Effie. — Do you pity me?

Helen.— Do fall in love, please! We'll just own this town.

Effie. — (*Laughing.*) With whom?

Helen. — Lord Poverty, of course!

Effie. — (*Seriously.*) I don't dare to ; I never met him until last summer.

Helen. — That don't count. I fell in love with Jack the very first time I saw him.

Effie. — He is absolutely without sentiment—except a love for music. (*Looks at* Helen.) Why! here I am telling you —

Helen. — (*Interrupting.*) I know everything.

Effie. — (*Surprised.*) Who told you?

Helen. — Lord Poverty. He loves you, and I—(*Aside.*) But I must n't tell.

Effie. — (*Laughing.*) He says, he loves me,—(*Seriously.*) but does he know the meaning of the word?

Helen. — He hasn't much sentiment, I admit; but you might rouse him—

Effie. — As Lord Poverty has made a confidante of you, I'll do the same. (*Shyly.*) I like him.

Helen. — A pretty girl like you ought to be in love with some one. I'd go mad, if I didn't love Jack.

Effie. — You dear child!

Helen. — (*Sighing.*) It takes all kinds of people to make a world.

Effie. — (*Putting her arms around* Helen.) Am I so very odd?

Helen. — (*Nods.*) Yes—You ought to love him. You'ar throwing away a good thing—that's what Jack calls it.

Effie. — (*Looking at* Helen. *Seriously.*) Let me tell you a story. A tiny girl; an orphan, scarcely ten, lived in Colorado with her brother, twelve years older. Then he died. Without relatives to care for her she would have—well—died too, I suppose; but for a young Englishman, her brother's friend. He caused her to be sent to England, cared for—and educated.

Helen. — (*Seriously.*) The little girl wasn't you, was it, Effie ?

Effie. — Yes.

Helen. — How noble of him. (*Earnestly.*) What is his name ?

Effie. — Bruce Buckingham. I have never seen him to remember him.

Helen. — Where is he?

Effie. — In South Africa!

Helen. — Is he nice looking ?

Effie. — I don't know.

Helen. — You've got his photograph?

Effie. — No. I never heard from him directly until my eighteenth year. Then I got my first letter; I answered it in a flood of tears, and sent him my photograph. Then came another letter, and an another, and they continued to come until eight months ago. In his last letter, he asked me not to marry, or promise to marry without his consent. Could you, under these circumstances, give your heart to the first man who would ask it?

Helen. — If the first man was Jack, I would. Where is Mr. Buckingham now?

Effie. — Somewhere in Africa. He said, in his last letter, that I wouldn't hear from him for a year or more.

Helen. — Was he fond of your brother?

Effie. — Very. The first time they met was in Selida.

Some cow-boys had insulted him. My brother seeing that he was a stranger took sides with him; revolvers were drawn and some one would have been killed, had they persisted in their insults. Afterwards they worked a prospect together. But the mine failed, my brother died, Mr. Buckingham went to South Africa.

Helen. — And you don't remember him?

Effie. — No, he was up in the mines most of the time; he was very young. At first the miners laughed at him because he was so odd, but after a while they just admired him. (*Enters* Poverty.)

Helen. — Say Effie there're heaps of strange things in the armour chamber. Oh I want to ask Lord Poverty about a painting I saw in one of the upper back rooms.

Poverty. — (*Who has heard* Helen's *remark.*) The modern painting?

Helen. — Yes, the large one.

Poverty. — " Her last dupe."

Helen. — I'm going up to see it again. (*Exit* Helen.)

Poverty. — (*Scrutinizing.*) Are you warm?

Effie. — I am a little chilly. ('*Putting on her wrap.*)

Poverty. — (*Looking at* Effie's *dress.*) Have you plenty of (*Hesitates.*) jackets and — (*Hesitates.*) strong clothes under that gown?

Effie. — (*Suppressing a smile.*) Plenty.

Poverty. — By the way Maloney, don't you find it awkward knocking about without a brother?

Effie. — (*Seriously.*) I wish I could recall my brother from above.

Poverty. — You should never think of releasing him. He'd never forgive you if you got him out. Now he's got nothing to do but to see God and fly around. Down here, he'd have to commence all over again dodging the brimstone chap. (*Changing the subject out of deference for* Effie's *feelings.*) You've got a fine look on to day.

Effie. — (*Smiling.*) Thank you; how is your Lord-ship?

Poverty. — A bit sentimental.

Effie. — Sentimental!

Poverty. — That's it.

Effie. — You! (*Laughs.*)

Poverty. — Why not? By the way, do you remember that bit of rhyming stuff, about a chap that went growling about, longing to meet another life?

Effie. — Another life?

Poverty. — Another girl—no—not another one, but the right one.

Effie. — (*Inquiringly.*) " There's another life I long to meet?"

Poverty. — That's it.

Effie. — "There's another, life I long to meet. Without whose life, my life is incomplete."

Poverty. — Clever, very clever. I've been wrapping the thing about on me tongue's end all day, but when I saw you I forgot it. What became of the wretch? Did he ever overtake her? (*Looking at* Effie.) Of course—to be sure.

Effie. — Perhaps.

Poverty. — " Without, whose, life, my life is incomplete." (*Approaching* Effie.) I know a chap, a good enough chap too, who wants to take your life.

Effie. — Take my life.   ·

Poverty. — Yes, and fill it with nonsense, and flowers and bonnets' and a horse or two. He hasn't money, but I think he can throw in the horses.

Effie. — (*Affecting indifference.*) Your friend ought not to marry without money.

Poverty. — Why not?

Effie. — The responsibilities following marriage.

Poverty. — (*Looking at* Effie.) The responsibilities!

Effie. — Yes.

Poverty. — Oh " *them* " things—they'll be provided for. The young Poverty's always start rich.

Effie. — Marriage is a serious affair, my lord.

Poverty. — Yes with the women. After all it's only a women question. The men bother around a bit on the day of the show—of course—that's it.

Effie. — (*Surprised.*) Marriage only a womens question?

Poverty. — (*Interrupting.*) Ah! but I mean the joining —away—together ceremonies, the veils and the gowns, and the lemon buds. (*Reflects.*) Lemon—(*To himself.*) That's not it—orange—that's it! (*To* Effie.) and the orange buds. But about the sentimental chap, the one who wants to complete his life by adding the right girl to it. He wants you, Maloney, you'll finish him. You see you're an American.

Effie. — (*Interrupting.*) Your friend can find plenty of American girls with wealth and beauty.

Poverty. — Ah, but you see—'its a joke on a chap to marry the wealthy ones. Their money is paraded too much. Ones marriage with them is awkward. 'Tis like taking over a bare back rider or a strong girl. Your friends laugh at you. You've got to neglect them afterwards to convince your set, that you've repented of your folly. But with a poor American girl or the ones with modest guineas 'tis different. There are warm hearts for such in England, even after the altar. (*Enters* Helen.)

Helen. — Oh Lord Poverty, Jack is putting on one of your ancestors iron suits.

Poverty. — Why not?

Helen. — Can I help myself too?

Poverty. — To anything.

Helen. — (*To* Effie.) There are lots of ladies wigs gowns, hats and everything. Go up and see them.

Effie. — Oh yes. (*Exit* Effie.)

Helen. — (*Advancing to centre of stage, confidentially.*) How are things working?

Poverty. — Me aunt is still suspicious.

Helen. — Of what?

Poverty. — Of the picalo affair with Maloney?

Helen. — Does Effie know that your aunt objets to her?

Poverty. — No, and she must never know it.

Helen. — Where's Benson today.

Poverty. — She'll be here. She's always nosing around. The devil herself could n't be worse!

Helen. — (*Indignantly.*) The devil herself!

Poverty. — It self—the devil itself— That's it.

Helen. — Are you and Effie going to play today?

Poverty. — I'm going to play but not with Effie—with a picalo chap from London—I've engaged him to play with me—to trick Benson. She'll go back to me aunt and clear me of the last affair.

Helen. — That's the way to scheme. Say Lord Poverty—don't you think we better tell Jack every thing right away?

Poverty. — Not until after the twentieth; too many cooks spoil the conspiracy. I must go, if you'll let me. The musician is in the small tower. (*Approaching to right driveway. Exit* Poverty.)

Helen. — Poor Lord Poverty, he's a real good fellow. (*Enters* Effie *with gown, wig, hat and mask.*)

Effie. — (*Laughing.*) Mr. Randolph wants you to put these on. He's coming right down. (Helen *puts gown, &c., on* Effie *helping her.*) He looks awfully funny. He's in armor.

Helen. — Like a real Knight. (*Enters* Jack *in armor with sword in hand. His coat tail sticks out behind—Exit* Effie.)

Jack. — (*Tragic strides.*) By the gibbeted carcass of the Silver Dwarf. I'll reckon curtly with him who calls thee daughter. Where is the tyrant?

Helen. — Sir Knight of Manhatten I implore thee, chide not my sire too harshly.

Jack. — Where's the tyrant?

Helen. — (*Tragically.*) The last time I saw him, he was girding up his trousers with silk suspenders.

Jack. — (*Seriously. Taking off his helmet and throwing it on stage.*) Look here Helen, what in the devil has your father got against me any way?

Helen. — (*Sorrowfully.*) Jack, don't spoil the fun.

Jack. — But what has he got against me?

Helen. — He says you're wild.

Jack. — He don't know me.

Helen. — He admits that, but Jack the trouble is he knows your father. (*Sorrowfully.*)

Jack. — Certainly! Your father and mine were great friends. They were boys together.

Helen. — (*Sorrowfully.*) Yes, but father says—(*Looking at* Jack.) You wont be offended will you Jack?

Jack. — Offended! N—o—

Helen. — He says that your father as a boy and young man was —the wildest—hellian in Westchester County, that his capacity for raising the devil was absolutely unlimited.

Jack. — I wasn't about to restrain the lad. I shouldn't suffer for his sins.

Helen. — (*Almost in tears.*) That of course I know, but Jack some one told father that for refined—double — distilled juvenile villiany, old Randolph Robins in the prime of his youthful " cusidness " couldn't hold a candle to his son Jack.

Jack. — You don't believe it, do you Helen?

Helen. — No I don't. (*Looking at* Jack.) He could hold a candle to you, couldn't he Jack?

Jack. — I know who told your father that.

Helen. — The wretch! Who, Jack?

Jack. — (*With doubtful air.*) Well I can't say that I know the man, but I know the county the stories came from.

Helen. — The county!

Jack. — Yes Westchester. I admit that these rumors against my character are traditional. Your father heard about me in Westchester, in Hudson where I lived summers until I was fourteen.

Helen. — I'd sue the county for slander.

Jack. — Would you? (*With faraway look.*)

Helen. — Yes I would, ruining a poor boy's character. (*With a look of wise indignation.*)

Jack. —(*With troubled looks.*) They might get one fact before the jury that would down me.

Helen. — What Jack.

Jack. — Now Helen I'll tell you. One indiscretion at Hudson gave me a bad name, an unsavory reputation.

Helen. — How old were you Jack?

Jack. — Thirteen.

Helen. — Tell me about it Jack, and head off your traducers.

Jack. — One Sunday I played poker—

Helen. — (*Interrupting*.) Father has done that.

Jack. — For pennies, that the ministers son stole from the contribution box.

Helen. — (*Interrupting*.) Did you know it Jack?

Jack. — Never suspected it.

Helen. — You didn't steal?

Jack. — 'Twasn't money.

Helen. — What did you take Jack?

Jack. -- Beer.

Helen. — (*Rolling up her eyes*.) Beer!

Jack. — Thirteen bottles of lager, I swiped them from fathers ice chest. I played the Milwaukies against the church funds.

Helen. — And it was found out?

Jack. — We were caught red handed.

Helen. — By whom.

Jack. — The undertaker.

Helen. — The undertaker?

Jack. — The game took place in his property.

Helen. — On his property, dear?

Jack. — In it darling. (*Sorrowfully*.) In his hearse. (Helen *nearly swoons*.) Now Helen! (*Puts his arm around her*.) My prize angle it was an unfashionable old thing with glass sides out of use, we had to, it commenced to rain.

Helen. — Oh! my, my heart! (*Looking at* Jack.) Jack promise me one thing—Promise me!

Jack. — (*Kissing her hand*.) Anything, anything.

Helen. — Don't sue the county.

Jack. — (*Seriously*.) Perhaps it's better to forbear. (*Reflecting*.) The moral delinquency of that Sabbath day shattered my earlier reputation. But I'll live it down.

Helen. — Oh Jack, we'll both live it down. Forget it —forget it.

Jack. — I never think of it, except when I see a hearse or a contribution box. (*Notes on the picolo heard from small tower.*)

Helen. — Hark! (*Listens.*) Benson—Benson. That's the signal. (*They make a rush for—the door—Find it locked.*)

Jack. — Spring lock! We're lost. (*Trys to get armor off.*) I can't get this devilish thing off! (*Helen takes wrap, &c., off—and makes an ineffectual effort to help Jack.*) No use—make for the tower—leave me—I'll take care of myself. (*Urging Helen.*) Go!

Helen. — Oh, Jack! (*Retires on path leading to ruined tower.*)

Jack. — (*Renewing effort to get armor off.*) I wonder who's trail Benson is camping on. (*Picolo duet,* Kling's " Two Little Finches " *now heard from small tower—Enters* Benson *looking thiner than in* first act. Jack *stands in vacant niche to right of door and assumes a statuesque attitude.* Benson *advances to centre of stage · listens to music and looks cautiously about her. Makes a note of time from watch. Looks at table—another note—Examines bottles—looks about—drinks. Looks about again—drinks—Disappears on path leading to small tower.* Jack *steps from niche—crosses stage to entrance on path* Benson *has taken—Looks after her.*)

Jack. — (*In low voice.*) She's peeping through the bushes to see who's in the tower. (*Retreating.*) Now she's returning—to the bottle—(*Laughs to himself—assumes former position in niche—*Benson *reappears—Looks about cautiously—Drinks—Listens to music.*)

Benson. — (*To herself pointing.*) His lordship. (*Enters* Mrs. Smile—*Music ceases.*)

Mrs. Smile. — (*Seeing* Benson.) For whom are you looking Benson.

Benson. — (*Bowing—A little unsteady.*) H—i—s—l—lordship.

Mrs. Smile. — Find Miss Rushfoot and you'll find his lordship, they're inseparable. (Benson *bows again—Utters a silly laugh and retires through arched entrance.*) I wonder if she knows that Poverty is engaged to Helen Rushfoot?

4

(Jack *nearly falls.*) I doubt it. Why dont Gordon come, he was to meet me here? (*Exit* Mrs. Smile *to right on roadway. Enters* Poverty *on path from right and* Helen *from left.*)

Poverty. — You understood my signal.

Helen. — Yes. (*Looking around.*) But where's Jack?

Poverty. — Me aunt's carriage is coming up the road— She's out for an airing. If she stops, you must see her.

Helen. — But suppose Jack should be around.

Poverty. — Send him up into the Armour chamber.

Helen. — Oh yes, I know —To see the painting! Her Last Dupe. (*Laughs. Enters* Bullock.)

Bullock. — (*Excited.*) Your lordship—Hif you please— A foreign looking tramp 'as nearly killed a boy on the roadside near the mote.

Poverty. — Who's the boy?

Bullock. — Hif Hi'm not mistaken me lud, 'tis Maxey

Helen. — Maxey!

Poverty. — (*Going toward arched entrance.*) Maxey!

Bullock. — Yes me lud.

Helen. — (*Aside.*) Maxey here! (*Exeunt* Poverty *and* Bullock *followed by* Helen.)

Jack. — (*Jumping from niche and taking off armour.*) Helen engaged! Well I'll be—(*Throwing armor on the stage.*) Did any one ever hear of a deed more foul—Engaged to Lord Poverty—Is n't this withering? I cant believe it—yet it must be true—the end has come—the combine is busted—I'm off for America. (*Goes to right.*) Her last dupe! (*Exit on roadway. Enters* Gower—*Arched entrance.*)

Gower. — (*Looking behind toward outer road.*) The boy must be badly hurt. (*Enters* Mrs. Smile *from left— Overhears* Gower *last remark.*)

Mrs. Smile. — Some one injured.

Gower. — Yes—Maxey!

Mrs. Smile. — (*Aside.*) Maxey here? (*To* Gower.) Has he been fighting?

Gower. — Bullock says the lad was assaulted.

Mrs. Smile. — By whom?

Gower. — A tramp—Some mendicant no doubt.

Mrs. Smile. — (*Aside.*) Strange—Maxey still here!

Gower. — The hunt was broken up. The liberal members of the club are out of the saddle and are voting for Maby to a man—Personally—I'm glad of it.

Mrs. Smile. — (*Scowling—Aside.*) I'm not. (*To* Gower.) How did it happen?

Gower. — Emery says that the ending was dramatic; that when nearing Monks Well, Rushfoot came dashing bye at a fearful pace. When rounding the road, that turns to the Giant Oak he fell; the impetus of his mad dash was so great that it swung his body around the bend of the road, out of view. Major Bradford hurried to the spot expecting to find him badly hurt, but Rushfoot had remounted. The major asked him if his fall was serious, but the colonel claimed that he didn't fall. This nettled Bradford who doesn't like the Yankees, you know; and he replied, by saying that the tongue of many a man had deceived him, but his eye—sight never had. Rushfoot retorted—with prevoking coolness, that he needn't boast of his eye sight, for he once owned a mule that could out spy him. Angry words followed. On reaching the club-house, Bradford sent the Colonel a hostile message. It's an odd fact that the hounds on reaching the spot where Rushfoot fell lost the scent, and the whips called them off.

Mrs. Smile. — This is news indeed. (*Noise on road from arched entrance.*) What new developement? (*Enters* Mrs. Maby *followed by* Bullock.)

Mrs. Maby. (*Alarmed. To* Bullock.) What's the trouble?

Bullock. — A tramp has nearly killed Maxey!

Mrs. Maby. — Maxey! Maxey! here?

Bullock. — Yes madam.

Mrs. Maby. — Impossible, he left with Sirao? (*To* Bullock.) Where is he?

Bullock. — They've carried him to the houter stable madam.

Mrs. Smile. — (*Aside.*) The boy will tell all, if he see

his lordship.   Poverty speaks Italian.   (*Enters* Poverty *followed by* Mr. Maby *and* Helen.)

Mrs. Maby. — (*To* Maby.) Is Maxey here?

Maby. — Yes.

Mrs. Maby. — What is the trouble?

Poverty. — (*To* Mrs. Maby.) Too serious for discussion here.

Mrs. Maby. — (*To* Poverty.) Tell me—tell me!

Poverty. — Maxey says that the Van Elfin is only a copy—that your husband has been cheated.

Maby. — (*To his wife.*) I don't believe him.

Mrs. Maby. — (*Excited.*) Impossible Lord Poverty! It can't be true.

Poverty. — The young chap said so, and then became unconscious.

Mr. Maby. — (*To* Poverty.) Did you talk to Sirao?

Poverty. — No—he was ugly.

Mrs. Maby. — (*Astonished.*) Sirao here too?

Poverty. — Yes he, struck Maxey. He was disguised, as a tramp.

Mrs. Maby. — (*To* Maby.) George, it can't be true. See Sirao at once! He'll surely tell the truth. Oh dear, I shall go mad!

Maby. — (*To* Mrs. Maby.) This alarm of yours, to say the least, is imprudent. (*To all.*) Accept my assurances, that Maxey has not told the truth. (*To his wife.*) In the name of all that's prudent, say nothing more until we know the fact.

Mrs. Maby. — But George!

Maby. — Do as I say, quiet your tears.

Mrs. Smile. — (*To* Gower.) Let us go.

Maby. — (*Overhearing* Mrs. Smile.) Please remain and listen for the guns.

Mrs. Smile. — Guns?

Mrs. Maby. — Yes—fired from Chapel Park.   One means victory, two that we have won by a majority of fifty or more.

Gower. — (*To* Mrs. Smile.) We must wait.

Maby. — (*To his wife.*) I'll make Sirao talk. (*Exit*
Mr. Maby.)

Mrs. Maby. — (*To* Mrs. Smile.) They must be mistaken. It cant be true. (*Enters* Rushfoot *wearing long
ulster, with capacious pockets. Left pocket bulging out and
carefully buttoned. Small slouch hat, the left leg of trousers
hanging from top of his boot. General appearance indicates
anxiety, haste and annoyance. Puts ulster on table after taking it off.*)

Rushfoot. — Think of it! On election day! imagine
it! A fox hunt to-day, or any day.

Gower. — The sport is inspiring.

Rushfoot. — Think of it! Women by the score. Men
by the hundreds, lackeys by the dozen, all on reckless
horse-flesh, preceded by a gang of big-fanged yelping
dogs, the whole outfit dashing pell mell, over ditches
and hedges, in devil—may—care unison, pursuing a fox,
a little fox. If it was a Mavrick Steer, or a long horned
Spanish bull, that would be different—but a little might
of a fox.

Mrs. Smile. — They follow the hounds in the States.

Rushfoot. — Not in my country, except those of the
smart set, who are in the process of transition from social obscurity, to the lower conditions of polite society.
But here, say my dear Poverty and Gower just a word,
if the ladies will excuse us. (*Ladies retire—To* Poverty.)
My boy I'm called out, challenged; (*To* Gower.) incited
to murder! (*Hands* Poverty *letter.*) Read the damned thing.

Poverty. — From Bradford.

Rushfoot. — (*Looking at* Gower.) Unless I apologise
the Major wants an immediate arrangement made for the
trial of our respective killing powers.

Gower. — You're putting the thing rather savagely.

Rushfoot. — (*Without appearing to have heard* Gower.)
Suppose I kill the major, snatch him from among his set;
why, without him, the whole outfit would n't be able to
corner brains enough, to accommodate the mental requi-
sites of a Piccadilly Masher. We don't fight—duels—in
my country; of course politicians do, public rejoicing

encourages such encounters, because they often prove
fatal. Mr. Gower hear me! (*Still looking at him.*) Cour-
ageous men have long since stamped out this medieval
need. It thrives to be sure, a little, in the sloughs of
tainted and giddy club life; but even there I'm pained to
say, the death rate isn't appalling. Country editors fight
too, but that's different. 'Tis fight or starve in such
cases, sometimes both, poor devils! Suppose I get killed
—cut off in the youth of my old age—damn it!—crowded off Gods green earth—by—(*To himself.*) a red—nosed,
red—headed English major—((*To* Poverty) I'll fight at
any time at any place! (*Cannon heard without.*) Hurrah!
George has won! Maby and Arbitration! Forever! (*Enters*
Helen, Mrs. Smile *and* Mrs. Maby.)

Helen. — (*To* Rushfoot.) Papa, didn't you hear a
cannon?

Rushfoot. — Yes.

Helen. — Oh! (*To* Mrs. Maby.) Brother George has
won.

Rushfoot. — (*Taking out his watch.*) Hark. (*Second
gun in heard.*)

Helen. — (*Listening.*) Second gun!

Rushfoot. — George has a majority of fifty or more.

Gower. — The credit of this victory is due to you,
Mr. Rushfoot.

Poverty. — (*Shaking* Rushfoot's *hand.*) Why not?

Gower. — (*To* Rushfoot.) How you did it, I can't
say; but you broke the hunt up.

Mrs. Smile. — (*Looking at* Gower.) Fortunately.

Gower. — Fortunately. (Rushfoot *whispers to* Gower.)
No! Ha—ha—ha, you did? Ha—ha—ha, that's great
regular cowboy. It's all over now; tell it. Ha—ha—
ha!

Mrs. Smile. — It's evidently a good joke, tell it.

Rushfoot. — When I heard of the hunt, I determined to
break it up—Mounting Fleeting John I located the
run, overtook and outstripped the party, hounds and all.
Near the old well, I saw the mite of a beast the gang
were after. When within twenty feet from him I

swung from my seat in the saddle and swiped him, as I passed.

Mrs. Smile. — Impossible!

Rushfoot. — (*Getting his ulster and throwing it over his arm.*) That's right—sure.

Poverty. — Have you any witnesses.

Rushfoot. — (*Taking the fox from his pocket.*) Only one.

Gower. — Thats's the fox—black tail and all.

Poverty. — You've won the day! (*Enters* Mr. Maby.)

Mr. Maby. — (*To his wife.*) Sirao admits that the Van Elfin is only a copy and he says that Maxey has destroyed the original.

Mrs. Maby. — Oh! (*Falls.*)

Rushfoot. — (*Kneeling and taking* Mrs. Maby *in his arms.*) Poor girl, the excitement of the day has overcome her.

— END OF SECOND ACT —

THE THIRD ACT

There's an elapse of three days between the Second and Third Acts.

The Scene is the large foyer hall of Devon House, Dorchester Oaks, *residence of* Mr. George Maby. *At the back, and between the right, and left entrances are two wide stair cases, ascending in segmental curves to a square landing, six feet from the floor. The stairs and landing have heavy carved balustrades. Between the stairs is a curved recess, in which rests, on a large easel, "* Van Elfin's Peace." *The painting stands perpendicularly. The top of the gilt frame is held by wooden cross piece, to prevent it from falling forward. Attached to the easel is a frame, elevated above the painting, and with cross bar, upon which are gas jets, with reflectors, to illuminate the canvas, as in the first act. The left entrance leads into interior hall, with door leading, it's supposed, to main front vestibule hall. The right entrance leads into another interior hall, with door leading, its supposed, to rear ,main entrance of house. On the left is a library with arched pillared entrance. Immediately opposite the library on the right is the drawing room, with entrance same as library.* Mrs. Maby *is seated at table looking ill and despondent.)*

Mrs. Maby. — Today is the eighteenth. (*Reflects.*) Still in darkness—the original undiscovered—what a dilemma! (*Enters* Maby, *with open letters in his hand.*)

Maby. — Our American mail.

Mrs. Maby. — Well?

Maby. — The great ore lead of the Slopper has broken off; but they find the same vein in the Extension. Extension shares are booming. (*To himself.*) Poverty has a block of three thousand — Extraordinary luck.

Mrs. Maby. — What do the detectives say?

Maby. — Nothing.

Mrs. Maby. — Nothing! Nor the solicitors?

Maby. — Nothing except that Sirao's bank account has been located and attached. The Italian was known to the Trafalgar Bank as Jacob Kaufmann.

Mrs. Maby. — The scoundrel!

Maby. — And a clever one. (*Offering letter.*) Read this.

Mrs. Maby. — (*Refusing letter.*) Please give me the substance.

Maby. — Sirao met Van Elfin in Rome last winter. He found the Dutchman in straightened circumstances and bought his " Peace " for four thousand pounds. Again in ninety four, at Madrid, he sold a Bartolomeo, but delivered a copy only. The fraud being detected, Sirao pleaded that the original had been accidently destroyed by fire immediately after the sale. The Spaniard, fearing the loss of his money, actually aided Sirao to get from the insurance compan the value of his painting. The original was afterwards sold in Paris. On that occasion he had two copies. One, he palmed off on the Spaniard; the other he burned, saving bits of charred canvas, to prove the loss of the original. I'm tempted to offer the wretch five thousand pounds to produce the original at once. It's no doubt in London.

Mrs. Maby. — Surely you wouldn't be weak enough— (*With spirit.*)

Maby. — (*Interrupting.*) But think of it—I'll be the laughing stock of all England—subjected to every kind of ridicule and malevolent criticism.

Mrs. Maby. — Even so, dont let the wretch blackmail you.

Maby. — (*With resignation.*) Well the end is at

hand. I'll notify Marlborough House at once that the
Celebration has been indefinately postponed. This even-
ing the committee of arrangements must know the fact.
Such an embarrassing position!

Mrs. Maby. — 'Tis indeed, you have my sympathy.
(*Exit* Mrs. Maby *left. Enters* Sirao *right. Officer stands
at entrance.*)

Maby. — Look! (*Pointing to painting.*)

Sirao. — Yes, Mr. Maby, the Van Elfin, Mr. Maby—
the Van Elfin.

Maby. — Where is the original?

Sirao. — My heart is not black—Mr. Maby—not
black.

Maby. — Answer my question!

Sirao. — I am an artist, not a cheat—Mr. Maby, My
heart—

Maby. — (*Interrupting.*) Don't persist in your decep-
tions; they'll avail you nothing. You wretch!

Sirao. — That's unkind Mr. Maby—you do me injury.
There's no profit in denunciation.

Maby. — Do you injury?—

Sirao. — I keep cool—I keep my temper.

Maby. — Think you, that England is without a pris-
on—that her laws will permit you to play the swindler
with impunity?

Sirao. — See me—Mr. Maby—I'm not excited.

Maby. — You are possessed of a prudent temper Jacob
Kaufmann.

Siaao. — (*Startled.*) " Jacob Kaufmann! " I don't
know the gentleman.

Maby. — The chairman of the Trafalgar Bank does.

Sirao. — (*Alarmed.*) Mr. Maby — listen — Maxey,
(*Clutching his hands.*) the devil Maxey—

Maby. — Stop! Abide by your own precept. "There's
no profit in denunciation."

Sirao. — He burned the original! (*Wrings his hands
and clasps them on his head.*) The great Van Elfin! Maxey
has destroyed it My God! the world has lost a canvas,
that allured the touch of a master. 'Tis burned! tis gone!

My great painting! 'Twas mine. My heart is not black—Mr. Maby. (*Beckons* Mr. Maby *to one side.*) I'll return *your* money—(*Confidentially.*) the insurance company will pay me. You, and the nice ladies, and the art critic can help me get *mine.* See my heart—Mr. Maby.

Maby. — (*With disgust.*) Sirao, understand me, I know your methods. You're in England not in Spain. You'll never swindle an insurance company here, as you did there. Once more—where is the original?

Sirao. — (*Agitated with conflicting emotions of wrath, and despers. Enters* Helen, *who stands at left entrance.*) You are a dev—damm—(*Grits his theet.*) Oh! Mr. Maby—please Mr. Maby—don't rob me, don't ruin me. My God, don't! What is there I can do, to convince you that I speak the truth. I will go to London with you, I will do anything. You are smart—you have wealth—take care—in refusing to believe me you rob yourself. (*Laughs.*) Time will tell. My God, I speak the truth!

Maby. — (*To* officer.) Take him away! Lodge him in jail to-night.

Sirao. — (*Excited.*) Damn, have a care—(Officer *approaches to hand-cuff him.* Sirao *clutches the air and grits his teeth, as the former comes near him.*) Go away, you beast! go away! Damn, you dog! (*Officer handcuffs him, after a struggle.*)

Maby. — Take him away!

Sirao. — (*With resignation.*) Hove a care! (*At right entrance.*) My last word—time will tell. Oh God! Mr. Maby, the picture is burned. (*Maby makes a motion to detective to take him away.*) Bah! (*To* Maby.) You damn! (*Grits his teeth and spits toward* Maby.) You devil! (*Stamps and spits again.*) Bah! (*Exit with* Officer. *Enters* Helen.)

Helen. — What a horrible man! Oh, dear! Really brother George, do you know I think that Maxey *has* burned the original.

Maby. — Out of revenge?

Helen. — Yes—every one now says, that Sirao has always been cruel to him. Poor little fellow.

Maby. — (*Reflects.*) Has Mrs. Smile called to-day.

Helen. — Why! no, the fog is so thick that you can't see a foot ahead of you.

Maby. — The fog is rising. (*To himself taking seat at table.*) Fog or no fog, Phellps must go to London to notify. His Royal Highness (*Writes.*)

Helen. — (*Aside.*) What's the matter with Jack? He hasn't answered the note I sent him by Bullock. (*Enters Taylor from right with brandy, &c., on tray-places some on table.*) That's a great way to keep the combine sweet— I'm mad—(Taylor *retires.*) and Jack Randolph will find it out! Poor boy, I haven't seen him since election day. But I'm mad. (*Exit Helen right. Enters Rushfoot left entrance, has overcoat on and looking generally dilapidated.*)

Rushfoot. — (*Turning his coat collar down.*) Say Maby —why in the devil don't your race move? Your old island is enveloped, more than half the time, in a mist, as dense as the expulsions of a smoke-stack.

Maby. — (*Pouring brandy into two glasses.*) You growl at our climate, but never at our brandy.

Rushfoot. — The blessed stuff - never! (*Taking glass.*) Your health! (*Drinks.*) That's good. Brandy is a trouble hunter—it's reaching Nothing on earth dispels the gloom of a man's soul (*An other glass.*) quicker than a glass—(*Drinks.*) than two glasses of good brandy.

Maby. — Devilish weather!

Rushfoot. — The fog is so thick, that I'll bet the Queen hasn't found her throne today, unless some one slept on it over night, and gave her a toot on a horn this morning.

Maby. — The fog nor the Queen doesn't concern me, but the Prince of Wales does.

Rushfoot. — Has he been notified?

Maby. — My friend Phillips leaves for London this afternoon. (*Goes toward right, exit. Enters Jack left.*)

Jack. — (*Goes up to Rushfoot, and grasps him warmly by the hand.*) I'm so glad to see you.

Rushfoot. — Evidently.

Jack. — (*Looking him over.*) Not a scratch, good! Did you pepper him?

Rushfoot. —. Who?

Jack. — The Britisher.

Rushfoot. — (*Hesitatingly.*) N—o.

Jack. — Too bad.

Rushfoot. — Who told you?

Jack. — (*Puts his fingers to his lips.*) I knew all about it. The Earth knows everything.

Rushtoot. — (*Looks at Jack and smiles. Helen appears at right entrance.*) Have a drink!

Jack. — Certainly! (*Helen alarmed.*)

Rushtoot. — Are you much of a drinker? (*Pouring out brandy for Jack.*)

Jack. — I can hold my own.

Rushfoot. — (*Still pouring.*) Say when?

Jack. — A little more!

Rushfoot. — (*Still pouring.*) How's that?

Jack. — Just a little more. (*Rushfoot continuing. Helen disappears.*) There, there—thanks.

Rushfoot. — Your health!

Jack. — (*Touching glasses.*) Pardon my curiosity, but (*Drinks.*) did you—(*Coughs violently.*) meet (*Coughs.*) Major Brad—(*Coughs.*) ford?

Rushfoot. — (*Laughs.*) You do hold your own, just about.

Jack. — (*With handkerchief to his eyes.*) Did you say — you met him?

Rushfoot. — No, we got lost in the fog.

Jack. — Too bad. I leave for America to-night. I cannot go without informing you, that the London press has been asked to investigate the Sirao swindle, and has sent reporters here to get the facts.

Rushfoot. — (*To himself.*) Poor Emma! (*To Jack.*) We want to keep the affair out of the press.

Jack. — Some one here, no doubt a woman, sent an anonymous letter to the London dailies, alleging that the gift of a copy of Van Elfin's Peace, and the intended ceremonies, incident to its presentation to the Arbitration League, were the devices of a Yankee woman, conceived for the sole purpose, of gaining social notoriety; that an exposure of the plot, would, no doubt, save the Prince of Wales from being inveigled into the scheme of honoring the occasion by his royal presence, and so forth, and so forth.

Rushfoot. — This is monstrous! Human malevolence has some limitations! You have been deceived, this story can't be true.

Jack. — I've got the letter in my pocket. A reporter believing me to be here, as the Earth's representative, on the same mission as himself, gave it to me to copy.

Rushfoot. — Can you let me have it, to show my son —in —law?

Jack. — Certainly, though I havn't copied it yet. (*Going toward left entrance.*) There is no impropriety in my doing that. It's only a devil's pigeon. (*Hands him letter.*)

Rushfoot. — Devil's pigeon? What's that?

Jack. — An anonymous letter. I'll return—and get it. (*Exit Jack.*)

Rushfoot. — "Devil's pigeon," (*Helping himself to another glass.*) that's good and new. Devil's pigeon— the foul hatch of a foul heart. (*Drinks.*) Life has its compensations. (*Enters Poverty, hat pulled down; coat turned up, and carries pistol case. Rushfoot takes him by the hand. With dignity.*) My lord, how did you lose me?

Poverty. — (*Surprised.*) Lose you?

Rushfoot. — Yes, my lord.

Poverty. — Of course that's it! You got out of the carriage, and didn't come in again

Rushfoot. — (*Smiling and putting his hand on* Poverty's *shoulder. Shows slight effect of the brandy.*) Listen, listen my boy! After getting out of the carriage, I—I looked about to see where we were. The fog was so thick, that I couldn't find the thing again. The real fact was this—(*Laughs.*) Poverty—my dear Pov—(*Laughing.*) I forgot which end of our carriage the horses were on. (*Laughing.*) Have a drink.

Poverty. -- Why not? (*They drink.*)

Rushfoot. — I'm sorry. I wouldn't have disappointed the major for one hundred thousand dollars.

Poverty. — Of course not. But you see, I fixed it.

Rushfoot — (*Surprised.*) Good! How?

Poverty. — After the doctor and I, the driver, and the horses and carriage lost you —

Rushfoot. — (*Laughs.*) That's good.

Poverty. — We knocked about for a bit, making at last for Rams Knoll. On the way we ran into Bradford's party, lost in a bank of fog, so thick that a bird couldn't flutter through it. I jawed Bradford's second, and asked him, why he hadn't met us. He replied, with some sort of foggy apologies, and then made a rush for the carriage to gab more, when he fell into a ditch. While they were hauling him out we moved on, saying you would meet Bradford in the morning, sa ne time and place.

Rushfoot. — (*Offering* Poverty *his hand.*) Shake my boy, shake! That's right. (*They shake hands.*) When you fabricate, do it with arrant grandeur. Now for one more! (Rushfoot *fills glasses.*)

Poverty. — Your health, why not?

Rushfoot. — (*Laughing.*) You did indeed fool the whole Bradford outfit. (*Holding up glass.*) As they say in Cripple Creek, here's that your life may be crowded with extravagant satisfactions and high grade indulgences.

Poverty. — (*Holding up glass.*) Here that the Major will miss you.

Rushfoot. — And that I'll hit him—(*They drink.*) weather permitting.

Poverty. — Of course. But he may apologize.

Rushfoot. — He ought to, he knows now, that I wasn't thrown.

Poverty. — He says that if you apologize, he will. Meet him half way, why not?

Rushfoot. -- Apologize—never!

Poverty. — Then it's fight?

Rushfoot. — Sure. I'll teach the Major that to challenge an American is a damned serious affair.

Rushfoot. — Come there's a plate for you. (*Going toward right entrance.*) Come.

Poverty. — Why not?

Rushfoot. — Apologize, no!

Poverty. — That's it. (*Exeunt Rushfoot and Poverty right. Enters Jack left.*)

Jack. — Things in this house are slightly crooked. (*Enters Helen from left.*)

Helen. — (*Overhearing Jack's remark.*) The affairs of the combine are not exactly straigt. (*With dignity.*)

Jack. — (*Aside.*) Her last dupe! (*Reflects.*)

Helen. — And what is Mr. Randolph thinking of?

Jack. — (*Aside.*) Isn't this refreshing! (*To Helen.*) Of a fool!

Helen. — Fool?

Jack. — Yes, one that's very close to you.

Helen. — (*Aside.*) He means brother George! (*To Jack.*) You're thinking of the painting, (*Tenderly.*) are n't you Jack?

Jack. — Yes. (*Aside.*) "Her Last Dupe."

Helen. — All this come of being too confident. (*Aside.*) Poor Jack, he'll have no more opportunities to criticise the Van Elfin. (*To Jack.*) Jack, Jack. "No more living fragments of the dead past."

Jack. — (*Aside.*) She's apeing on me. (*To Helen going toward left entrance.*) I'm off for America—the combine is forever dissolved—you and Lord Poverty can't fool me any longer. Marry the Britisher and be happy.

Helen. — Jack — !

Jack. — (*Interrupting.*) "Your last dupe." (*Exit Jack left.*)

Helen. — (*Following Jack.*) Jack, Jack. Come back! Oh Heavens! Jack has discovered the mock engagement. (*Enters Effie.*)

Effie. — Why! As Mr. Randolph rushed passed me, he said he was going to America.

Helen. — (*In despair.*) Effie pity me—pity me!

Effie. — Helen—what is the matter.

Helen. — (*Aside.*) Jack thinks I love Lord Poverty. (*To* Effie.) I see it all. (*Enters* Poverty *left.*) I see it all. (*Walking up and down stage.*) I feel like a lioness, that's lost her only—her only Jack. Oh dear, my head —I've lost it—My mind is going—I'm mad!

Poverty. — Mad—of course.

Helen. — Lord Poverty, you are the cause of it. Your love for me was only pretence.

Poverty. — Pretence of course.

E fie. — (*Alarmed.*) What! Impossible!

Helen. — (*Going toward right entrance.*) What a fool I've been. (*Exit Helen.*)

Poverty. — (*Looking at* Effie.) Is the situation clear to you?

Effie. — Yes. (*Sighing.*)

Poverty. — Is it now?—Fancy!

Effie. — Quite clear.

Poverty. — What is the muss?

Effie. — (*Slowly.*) Have you ever pretended to love Helen?

Poverty. — Of course—to be sure.

Effie. — And you didn't?

Poverty. — How could I love her and you at the same time?

Effie. — I am sorry to hear—

Poverty. — (*Interrupting.*) I've been making an ass of myself. You see, I've been after the money—(*Aside.*) and Heatherstone.

Effie. — Oh Lord Poverty!

Poverty. — Why not—I might as well have it as anyone else. (*Enters* Benson, *looking thiner than in the second act; hands* Poverty *a letter, bows again in most humble manner and retires.*) Would you mind, if I took a look at this? (*Goes to right of stages commences to read and comment to himself.*) Here me aunt raises the devil. (*Turns over a page.*) Here's the milk of the cocoanut. (*Reads.*) " Believing that your faults have been exaggerated, I, in consequence, concluded on the twentieth not to disinherit

5

your whole line, but instead, to provide for the well-fare of your successor, should you marry Mrs. Rushfoot or an other. Personally you inherit nothing—My entire estate, both personal and real, is left to the fir t male issue of your body. " Lady Hamilton." " The first male issue." 'Twould be a joke if the first was a girl. (*Reflects*.(Another girl, another joke. Fine assets An aunt of mine had thirteen girls—thirteen—(*Reflects*.) that's it. (*To* Effie.) You see I've been check—mated. Let her keep her money--the baby will have it. I'll tell you the whole thing—

Effie. — The baby!—(*Alarmed*.) Lord Poverty—I must go. (Mr. Maby *appears at right entrance*.)

Mr. Maby. - (*Excited*.) Your lordship.

Poverty. — (*Looking at* Maby.) Ah, yes.

Mr. Maby. - Maxey has regained consciousness—He's talking in Italian.

Poverty. — Is he in the lodge?

Maby. — No, we removed him into the servant's quarters.

Poverty. — And you want me?

Mr. Maby. — If you please.

Poverty.— (*To* Effie.) I must talk 'o you; wait please. (*Exeunt* Poverty *and* Maby.)

Effie. — The situation isn't so clear to me now. (*Reflecting*.) I don't dare to think. Oh dear! I have loved—I'm frightened, I must go. (*Enters* Jack.)

Jack. — I must have that letter. Oh! pretending to love me, when she loved Lord Poverty. (Effie *surprised, coughs to attract* Jack's *attention*.) Miss Revere! Did you get on to—I mean, did you overhear any of my remarks?

Effie. — I'm afraid, I did.

Jack. — I thought I was alone.

Effie. — Pardon me, but—but—

Jack. — (*Aside*.) She's tumbled. (*To* Effie.) Miss Revere, you are an American, so am I—you're in trouble, so am I—I know it. I've been aped on, and so have you.

Effie. — Aped on?

Jack. -- Yes—monkeyed with—made a fool of. Lord Poverty has pretended to love you, hasn't he?

Effie. — Assume he has.

Jack. — (*Confidentially.*) He cares no more for you, than Helen Rushfoot does for me. He's a deceiver, and Helen Rushfoot is—well—

Effie. — (*Interrupting.*) I'm horrified!—It can't be true!

Jack. — Do you know the situation? Yet, I have loved that girl.

Effie. — (*Faintly.*) Let me get out into the open air.

Jack. — (*To* Effie.) My soul is stirred with such—(*To himself.*) damnable emotions—I'll jump the game now and send for the letter. (*Aside.*) "Her last dupe." (*Exeunt* Effie *and* Jack *left. Enters* Maby *from right followed by* Helen.)

Maby. — (*With open letter in his hand.*) Astounding!

Helen. — (*Aside.*) Oh, my head! (*To* Maby.) What does Emma say?

Maby. — Nothing.

Helen. — Nothing? (*Aside.*) Poor Jack! What a fool I've been.

Maby. — She looked at the letter, and recognizing the handwriting of Lizzie Smile, recoiled at the sight of her friend's treachery. I must go. Maxey relapsed, didn't he?

Helen. — Yes before Lord Poverty reached the chamber.

Maby. — I am going to the hotel to see **Mr.** Randolph. Something must be done to avert a newspaper scandal. (*Starts to left, hesitates, and then goes to the right.*) First, I'll see how your father is getting on with Sirao. (*Exit.*)

Helen. — (*Looking into the vestibule hall.*) Some one coming. Oh, I must see Jack I must see him and explain. (*Exit right. Enters* Mrs. Smile.)

Mrs. Smile. — (*Looks, about her.*) Foggy· (*Looks, at pictures taking a position that commands view of both entrances.*) The shock should have come after and not before their

celebration.   Fate still scowls —on the Maby's.   (*Laughs.*)
I wonder if the reporters have been here yet? Emma Maby will find perchance, that a fearless press, knows how
to blister the hearts of even the audacious.   Think of
these Yankee millionaires; they come among us,—throw
their money here, and elsewhere, as a butcher would—
shy a bone to a scurvey cur, and fancy forsooth, that
the gates of royalty, should be thrown open to them.
Oh! this sensitive friend of mine.   She may yet learn
that the road that leads, from the planes of social medio-
craty, to the summit of royal favor, is beset with perils.
(*Enters* Mrs. Maby, *very feeble, grasping objects as she advances*
Mrs. Smile *starts to go toward her, but an indefinable gesture
from* Mrs. Maby, *causes her to forbear.*)

Mrs. Smile. — I am sorry Emma to find you so ill.

Mrs. Maby. — Only a nervous spell.

Mrs. Smile. — Anxiety, poor girl.

Mrs. Maby. — (*Approaching the picture.   Gazes at it
while supporting herself by grasping a chair.*) How beautiful! (*Putting her handkerchief to her eyes and silently weeping.*) Come! (*Extending her hand backward without moving
her body.*) Come! (*Pulls her hand back as though horrified
at her act.* Mrs. Smile *not seeing her extended hand remains
motionless.*)   Beyond the river, (*Weeps.*) – two maidens
walk hand in hand —the taller one looks like —(*Turns and
gazes at* Mrs. Smile.) How beautiful you were¡ (*Weeps.*)
And oh, how I loved you! (*Turns again to the painting.*)

Mrs. Smile. — (*To herself.*) Does she suspect? Impossible!

Mrs. Maby. — The smaller one · how trustingly she
gazes into the eyes of her fair companion.   (*Weeps.*)

Mrs. Smile. — Why Emma! you're almost in a state
of collapse.

Mrs. Maby. — Not now —these tears strengthen me.
(*Stands without support.*)

Mrs. Smile. — Emma, you are too ambitious.

Mrs. Maby. — (*Looking at her handkerchief, that the
twists, nervously in her hand.*) No—no, only unhappy.

Mrs. Smile. — You ought to be happy.

Mrs. Maby. — (*Looking at* Mrs. Smile.) Ought to be happy ? (*Greatly moved*.)

Mrs. Smile. — In your present condition, you'll be unequal to the task of entertaining royalty; your nerves—

Mrs. Maby. — (*Interrupting. With spirit*.) My country women require no nerve, nothing but heart, to entertain a prince, without it they could n't entertain a pauper.

Mrs. Smile. — (*Sarcastically*.) English women esteem it a high privilege to act the hostess to a guest as exalted as his Royal Highness. You Americans may regard such presence, as a mere incident to your generous spread— giving the matter no farther thought, than that of telling the butler to drop an extra plate on the table.

Mrs. Maby. — (*With spirit*.) Should the Prince of Wales ever sit at my " generous spread," his coming shall not be signalized by the dropping of an extra plate on the table, nor shall I, though the wife of a British subject, drop my self respect, as though it were a dirty apron, to cringe, stammer and scrape before him though he were twice a prince, king or emperor.

Mrs. Smile. — As the wife of a British subject you will discover that the homage due to his Royal Highness is prescribed by inexorable canons, the infraction of which to say the least will render you open to the common criticism that - (*She hesitates.*)

Mrs. Maby. — That what!

Mrs. Smile. — " That court obeisance, gauls only "—

Mrs. Maby. — Yes ?

Mrs. Smile. — " The American parvenu."

Mrs. Maby. — (*Indignantly*.) Epigrammatic slander has no terrors for me. Let me deal in honest words, words that have not been whipped into a smart phrase, by the groveling sycophants of royalty, but words that proclaim the nobility of human intelligence and those words are, madame that within the sovereignties of the Great Republic, we bend the knee to none, but God, and our mothers.

Mrs. Smile. — Why Emma! I marvel at the sublimity of your spirit. After all you can't blame one for sticking up for one's own country. Perhaps I made a mistake, in presuming upon the friendship of years to hint, that after all, social discontent is but the heart burn of wealth.

Mrs. Maby. — Socially, I ask for nothing, but what belongs to me. What you are pleased to call my social aims, I call my social rights. Englands gentry are wisely conscious of a superior class to their own—upwards then is my aim—'tis there I'll find my equals. (*Falls into a chair.*) I sent for you, this morning to--but it doesn't matter, and in fact, I regret—that—you came. (*To herself.*) I can't accuse her. (*Enters* Helen *excited.*)

Helen. — (*Excited.*) Maxey—!

Mrs. Smile. — Emma, can I do anything for you?

Mrs. Maby. — (*Without looking at her.*) Yes, step into the drawing room.

Mrs. Smile. — (*Looks at* Helen *then at* Mrs. Maby.) Certainly. (*Goes to drawing room entrance. Aside.*) Strange, very strange! (*Retires.*)

Helen. — Maxey has regained consciousness!

Mrs. Maby. — Who's with him?

Helen. — Lord Poverty.

Mrs. Maby. — Has he spoken?

Helen. — Not yet. He sat up in bed, looked about and then fell back and began to cry.

Mrs. Maby. — Poor boy!

Helen. — (*Looking toward drawing room door.*) Madame Treachery, I hope never to see your face again. (*Exit* Helen. *Enter* Rushfoot. *right.*)

Rushfoot. — (*To* Mrs. Maby.) The painting is destroyed.

Mrs. Maby. — George insists, that Sirao is playing his Spanish trick on us.

Rushfoot. — He's wrong; Sirao could no more deliver Van Elfin's Peace to him, than an assassin could call from the grave, the victim of his treachery.

Mrs. Maby. — It's no use. (*Enters* Mr. Maby)

Mr. Maby. — (*Excited.*) The reporters insist upon seeing the painting; they're coming over directly. There must be no excitement. I've admitted nothing; said nothing. (*To* Rushfoot.) Did you get anything out of Sirao.

Rushfoot. — Enough to convince me, that he's telling the truth. (*Enters* Helen *right entrance.*)

Helen. — (*Excited.*) Brother George, Maxey is up!

Mrs. Maby. — Up?

Helen. — Yes, and dressed. Taylor is taking him down. Here he comes! (*Enters* Maxey, *pale and weak. His head is bandaged and a silk shawl is thrown over his shoulders. He is supported by* Taylor, *who walks behind him. He jabbers to* Poverty, *who has entered with him, in* Italian, *and in broken* English.)

Maxey. — Dove mi porti? (*Where are you taking me*)?

Poverty. — Dove ti porto? Dai tuoi amici. ("*Where am I taking you.*" *Among your friends.*)

Maxey. — Mi porti da mia sorella in Italia. (Take me to my sister in Italy.)

Poverty. — Take you to your sister. Of course—we'll send you to her. (Da tua sorella? Di certo ti manderomo da lei.)

Maxey. — (*Sinks to the floor.*) Mamma mia! (Mother!) (*Cries.*)

Poverty. — (*To* Mrs. Maby.) The lad calls for his dead mother. He's hardly conscious. (Mrs. Maby *weeps.*)

Maxey. — (*Starts. Looks about him; sees the painting. In terror.*) Mi amazzerà! Aiuto aiuto! (He will kill me! Hide me!) (*Trys to stand.*)

Poverty. — Sirao, won't kill you; we wont let him. You needn't hide. (Sirao, non ti amazzerà, non c'é bisogno di aiuto.)

Maxey. — (*Looks at* Poverty *scrutinizing his face.*) No, Lei non e'. (No—o. You're not—)?

Poverty. — No. I'm not Sirao. (No, non sono Sirao.)

Maxey. — (*Sees* Mrs. Maby.) Lada! lada! (*Points to picture.*) Origa! origa!

Rushfoot. — He says this in the original.

Mr. Maby. — (*Points to painting.*) This? (*Goes up to painting and puts his finger on it.*) This? (*Nods.*) This?

Maxey. — (*Shakes his head.*) Bada! bada! (*Points again to painting.*) Origa!

Rushfoot. — First he says it's the original, and then he says it isn't.

Poverty. — (*Talks to Maxey, who has become very weak, but rational. All gather about to hear the outcome. To* Rushfoot.) The thing is all right. (Poverty *looks toward painting.*) Of course—why not? (*Speaks a few hurried words to* Rushfoot *and then to* Maby.)

Rushfoot. — (*Hastily examines back end of frame.*) That's right! (*To* Poverty.) Sure!

Mr. Maby. — (*Excited, pulls out his watch.*) The train leaves in twenty minutes! (*To* Taylor.) Rush to the stable! tell Harry to mount, and ride for his life to the station, have Phillips return at once. Quick! Not a moment to lose!

Mrs. Maby. — (*Who has been standing near left entrance.*) George, the reporters are here! (*Excited.*)

Mr. Maby. — The reporters! (*To* Rushfoot.) Take Maxey into the drawing room, quick!

Rushfoot. — (*Taking* Maxey *in his arms.*) Come, my boy, you're among friends. (*Exit carrying* Maxey. *Enters* Sirao, *handcuffed to* Police constable, *at right entrance.*)

Police constable. — (*To* Maby.) The prisoner wants a word with you, sir.

Mr. Maby. — This stupid constable! Get Sirao out of here!

Sirao. — (*To* Maby.) My heart, Mr. Maby—Mr. Rushfoot will tell you that my heart—(*Enter reporters.*)

Maby. — (*To* Poverty.) Get Sirao out; don't let the handcuffs be seen!

Poverty. — Of course. (*Taking newspaper from the table. Takes* Sirao *and constable by manacled arms from behind, throws paper in front of him, so as to conceal handcuffs. Whispers to* Sirao *and officer. To* Maby.) Just a moment. (*They continue to bow, as they back toward right entrance.*) Why not? (*Exeunt. Enters* Rushfoot.)

Reporter. — If you will pardon us, Mr. Maby, we failed to gather from our last interview with you, at the hotel, whether you were in possession of Van Elfins master piece or only a copy.

Maby. — (*Pointing to painting*.) There, gentlemen, is the copy. (*Enters* Poverty.)

Poverty. — (*To* reporters.) Of course.

Rushfoot. — (*Drawing out copy from the end of frame and exposing the original.*) And here gentlemen, is the original! (*The colors of original are brighter. The illumination of painting, by turning on gas of all the jets at the same instant, is greater.*)

Poverty. — To be sure.

Mr. Maby. — Just a little surprise to entertain our friends. (*Looking at* Mrs. Smile.)

Poverty. — Why not?

Mrs. Smile. — A surprise indeed. (*Laughing long and loud.*)

— END OF THE THIRD ACT —

THE FOURTH ACT

_____

There's an elapse of three days between the Third and Fourth Acts.

_____

The Scene *is the large drawing room in* Poverty Castle, *five miles from* Dorchester Oaks. *Facing the audience, is an arched entrance, with pillars on each side, leading into large hall. On the left of stage, is an entrance leading into the modern wing of castle, and on right, another entrance to the deserted quarters. The room is a cheerless one. The walls are decorated, with portraits of women in court trains, knights in armor, hunting scenes, &c., &c. Ancient armor, swords and battle axes are distributed about the room. The portraits, on the wall, are hung in an irregular manner, tilted to right and left. Large ancient table stands in centre of room, with chairs, strewed about, without pretense to order. The appearance of the room suggests dust and cobwebs.* Poverty *is discovered, sitting on end of table, learning against an old chest, playing a low soft melody on the flute. The floor and table are strewn with papers and documents that he has been taking from chest.*

Poverty. — (*Standing—Examines papers.*) Me assets are low. (*Takes another paper from box.*) God don't think much of money, or He'd (*Looks in box.*) give more of it to his best chaps. (*Looking for another paper.*) Now and then, a decent man has millions (*Examining box.*) dumped on him. (*Looking at audience.*) Too much of the stuff is awkward, they tell me. You can't chuck junks of it, at the howl ot every beggar, neither can you bag it all; without being called an ass in the first instance, and a hog in the second. This was the wise observation of an American millionaire, and a fine chap he was—they tell me. Personally, I rather be a (*Examining box.*) hog, and wallow in the dough, than an (*Examining box.*) ass, and eat the thistles of an envious world (*Throws papers in box, and crams them down.*) It's not there. (*Pulls bell cord. Cracked bell rings with a noisy ding.*) Where are me shares. (*Enters Bullock.*) Bullock—where are me other assets?

Bullock. — Hin the Harches Tower; me lud.

Poverty. — Bring them here—take these out.

Bullock. — Himmediately me lud. (*Places box on floor. Puts documents, that have fallen on the table, into box and stamps on them.*)

Poverty. — (*Watching him.*) That's right, Bullock—be careful—don't lose any.

Bullock. — Pardon the observation, me lud. Hi've never lost ha paper since Hi've 'ad charge hof the family harchives.

Poverty. — You're careful, Bullock. Of course.

Bullock. — Hi 'opes Hi ham, me lud. (*Takes box up, starts to go, then hesitates.*) Hif your ludship pleases, you've forbidden me to henter the Harches Tower, on haccount of the setting 'en.

Poverty. Do you mean, Nancy?

Bullock. — No me lud. Nancy 'as 'er nest hin the mahogany wardrobe hof the state chamber. 'Tis Queen Moll, that's hin the Harches Tower.

Poverty. — Fancy? I thought it was Nancy. Don't bother about Queen Moll, she's not game.

Bullock. — Very well, me lud. (*Starts to go.*)

Poverty. — Bullock, keep the cat out of the of the state chamber.

Bullock. — Hi 'aven't seen the cat, me lud, for some days. (*Starts again.*)

Poverty. — Bullock!

Bullock. — Yes, me lud.

Poverty. — Get another cat—the rats must be kept down.

Bullock. — Himmediately, me lud. (*Exit with box. Enters* Helen *from right entrance.*)

Helen. — Why don't Jack come;

Poverty. — (*Examining papers, he takes from drawer.*) He'll be here. Why not?

Helen. — (*Seriously.*) I've done something you'll like.

Poverty. — Of course—

Helen. — (*Looking at* Poverty.) Effie is coming here today.

Poverty. — Is she now!

Helen. — 'Twas good of you to intercept Jack at Liverpool for me.

Poverty. — To be sure. You see he registered at the Adelphi. Finding him out, I dropped him a line, saying that we were all going to America, on the next steamer, and asking him to return to Dorchester Oaks, and go with us.

Helen. — What did Jack say in his answer? Please tell me every word.

Poverty. — He said he thought, you were trying to pull my—(*Looks in drawer.*) hand for a title.

Helen. — (*With surpressed laugh, but with mock seriousness.*) Are you sure, he said hand.

Poverty. — (*Looking at* Helen.) No, no, that's not it, 'twas leg—of course. And he said he was sorry to hear, that you were (*Looking at paper.*) dying.

Helen. — Dying?

Poverty. — Yes—dying on account of him.

Helen. — Lord Poverty! you didn't write him any such stuff, as that in your letter did you?

Poverty. — I told him, that you were mushed on him.

Helen. — Oh! Don't, don't! (*Wringing her hands and laughing.*) It isn't mushed, it's m-a--s-h-e-d, mashed!

Poverty. — Yes – why not?—of course. But you see

it's too late now, I wrote it m-u-s-h-e-d,—mushed. It's quite the same—why not?

Helen. — Oh dear me! All this humiliation, all this sorrow, comes from the awful mistake we made in not telling—Jack everything.

Poverty. — Of course—I quite see that.

Helen. — Jack is so jealous.

Poverty. — Jealous, that's it.

Helen. — If Jack had known, that it was only a game to deceive Benson, he would have enjoyed it so—so much.

Poverty. — So much? Of course.

Helen. — Oh, I wish Jack would come! (*Seriously.*) Do you know, I've been all over your castle.

Poverty. — Have you, now?

Helen. — Lord Poverty—your roof leaks.

Poverty. — Does it?

Helen. — Yes, everywhere, except that end. There is no roof on that end. (*Pointing.*) Why don't you stop the leaks at this end? (*Pointing.*)

Poverty. — You see, the Povertys have always had a weakness for ventilation.

Helen. — (*Touching table, and then wiping dust off her finger with handkerchief.*) Is your house-keeper a very competent woman?

Poverty. — The last one was—I've none now.

Helen. — Has she been gone long?

Poverty. — Five years, I think.

Helen. — (*Aside.*) So do I. (*Looking about and shuddering.*) Lord Poverty, you wont be offended, if I ask you a question—will yon?

Poverty. — Nonsense!

Helen. — You wont think me ill bred.

Poverty. — Not at all—go on.

Helen. — If you should ever marry Effie, would you take her, to live here.

Poverty. — Of course—why not? I'd live in a garret with Maloney—if it leaked. You know, I must have ventilation.

Helen. — Where would you keep your hens then ?

Poverty. — We'd eat the hens—why not!

Helen. — (*Looking at portraits.*) Who were these? (*Pointing to knights.*)

Poverty. — Povertys.

Helen. — And the ladies?

Poverty. — More Povertys.

Helen. — (*Pointing to portrait.*) Don't you think, that knight is a little skewed.

Poverty. — He was, I think—I'm—

Helen. — (*Laughing.*) No, no! I mean the portrait. It's higher on this side than on the other. (*Pointing.*)

Poverty. — (*Looking.*) Fancy! (*Loud knocking at the outer door of front entrrnce.*) A caller, and Bullock is not here, (Poverty *disappears for an instant and then returns.*) Mr. Maby—

Helen. — Is Jack with him?

Poverty. — I'll see. (*Retires. Knocking continnes. Poverty is heard, calling to wait a minute. Noise of falling boards. Enters Maby, with dust on his coat, handkerchief in hand, wiping dust of his face, followed by Poverty.*)

Maby. — Who--(*Sneezes.*) was—(*Sneezes.*) the last man who entered that door? (*Sneezes.*) I'm nearly choked. *Turns and looks at entrance.*)

Poverty. — The sheriff.

Maby. — And the man before him?

Poverty. — Another sheriff, I think—

Maby. — Are you sure it wasn't William the Conqueror. (*Laughs.*) Well, well, my lord! (*Looking about him.*) how are you?

Poverty. — Busy. I'm straightening matters up, to go to America. (Helen *disappears through arched entrance.*

Maby. — (*Looking about.*) Straightening matters up eh? You'll be busy then for the winter.

Poverty. — A few hours.

Maby. — (*Laughing.*) You're booked for Saturday, yes, —Why did you let Rushfoot get into this scrape?

Poverty. — The duel?

Maby. — Yes, you're liable to arrest, at any moment. In fact the police are stirring.

Poverty. — Of course—So are we.

Maby. — Is Bradford badly hurt?

Poverty. — Cheek grazed, and part of his ear gone. Only one shot.

Maby. — Where is Bradford?

Poverty. — On the way to Belgium. When we quit, they'll not have evidence enough to justify a warrant. In six months the affair will be forgotten.

Maby. — Where are the folks?

Poverty. — In the Anne repacking their luggage.

Maby. — The " Anne "?

Poverty. — Yes, the Queen Anne, the wing—the modern end. (*Pointing.*)

Maby. — Modern! (*Laughing to himself.*)

Poverty. — Built in seventeen and eighteen.

Maby. — From the way Mr. Rushfoot got out of Devon House, I should think he'd need to repack. (*Laughing.*) I must see Mrs. Maby. By the way, you've heard about the big strike on the Extension.

Poverty. — Yes, I'm looking for me shares. (*Enters Helen.*)

Maby. — The shares closed yesterday at twenty seven pounds.

Poverty. — (*To himself.*) I must find me shares.

Helen. — (*Aside.*) Where is Jack ? (*To* Maby.) Brother George did anyone call after we left?

Maby. — Noboby—

Helen. — (*Aside.*) Oh dear!

Maby. — Except Mr. Randolph and Miss Revere. They rode over with me. (*To* Poverty.) Your driveway, my lord, in the inner court, is in bad shape, it needs repairing.

Poverty. — New dirt—of course.

Maby. — Mr. Randolph and Miss Revere jumped out to save themselves from being dumped.

Helen. — (*Aside.*) Jack and Effie here. I'll get my hat. (*Goes to left entrance.*)

Maby. — (*To* Helen.) Wait—do you know the ramifications of the " Anne " (*Laughs to himself.*)

Helen. — Follow me.

Maby. — (*To* Poverty.) My lord Extension shares twenty seven pounds! (*Laughs. Exeunt* Helen *and* Mr. Maby.)

Poverty. — Fancy' I've three thousand shares. I'm no hand at figures. (*Reflects.*) The noughts from three thousand leaves three; three times seven is twenty one —I've used the noughts and the seven up, Three times twenty is sixty and twenty one are eighty one—with the used up noughts added, make eighty one thousand, and then the pounds! That's it! eighty one thousand pounds. But I can't find me shares. (*Enter* Jack *and* Elfie *through the arched hallway.* Jack *appears doubtful as to where the entrance leads. Looks in.*)

Jack. — (*Without seeing* Poverty.) This is—

Effie. — (*Looking.*) What?

Poverty. — (*Hearing* Effie's *voice.*) Come in Maloney! why not?

Jack. — (*With dignity.*) I'm here Lord Poverty.

Poverty. — Of course — you're as good as your word.

Effie. — I'm out of breath.

Poverty. — (*Rings;* Effie *starts,* Jack *smiles.*) It takes the wind out of one to shank Poverty Hill. (*To* Effie.) You'll have some water?

Effie. — No, no thank you. (Poverty *rings twice.*) I really don't care for any.

Poverty. — Of course. Two bells mean " don't come Bullock."

Jack. — (*Aside.*) I wish some of our lord-cracked American girls could see the inside of Poverty Castle. (*Laughs.*)

Effie. — (*To* Poverty.) Where is Miss Rushfoot?

Poverty. — This way—(*Pointing to left entrance.*) I'll show you. (*Going toward left entrance.*)

Effie. — Thank you.

Poverty. — If Mr. Randolph will pardon me

Jack. — (*Who has been looking at pictures.*) Certainly. (*Exeunt* Elfie *and* Poverty. *Enters* Helen *from arched hall way.*)

Helen. — (*Doesn't see* Jack.) Oh dear! where is he? (*Sees* Jack—*starts.*) My!

Jack. — (*Sarcastically.*) Looking for Lord Poverty no doubt.

Helen. — No I'm not looking for Lord Poverty, but for my great big ninny John Randolph Robins Jr. (*Kisses him.*)

Jack. — (*Indifferently.*) Thank you.

Helen. — (*Looks at* Jack.) For what, the kiss or the complement?

Jack. — I don't want you to kiss me again.

Helen. — I will. I'll kiss you as much as I chose.

Jack. — (*Working his foot.*) I know how to suffer.

Helen. — So do I· Horrible! (*Making faces.*) you've been smoking.

Jack. — His lordship don't smoke.

Helen. — He smokes too—It's perfectly awful.

Jack. — What?

Helen. — The odor of an English pipe. Jack, you're jealous.

Jack. — You're mistaken.

Helen. — Not jealous?

Jack. — No, not jealous, but aped on.

Helen. — (*Seriously.*) You've been wronged Jack, but not aped on.

Jack. — I've been monkied with, any way.

Helen. — That of course, I know, but not aped on.

Jack. — (*With indignation.*) Monkied with! Have I been brought back from Liverpool to have my lacerated heart anointed with vitrol?

Helen. — Now Jack, you stop! You joined me in my exile, didn't you? and why? Because you knew I loved you and of course, anybody could see. that you loved me. We wanted to be together; to do so, you had your hoodwinking to do, I had mine—Lord Poverty had his. I was to pretend to love Lord Poverty, in order that he might love Effie under cover. Lord Poverty was to make out that he loved me, in order that you and I might—

Jack. — Might what?

Helen. — Spoon it—without being suspected. That's the English of it.

Jack. — Why didn't I get the tip?

Helen. — (*Snappishly.*) This was our blunder you should have been in the scheme but Lord Poverty throught it imprudent to let you or Effie know.

Jack. — (*Approaching Helen.*) Helen dear!

Helen. — (*Retreating.*) Jack Robins you keep away from me. (*Affecting to cry.*) Take your old steamer and go to America! (*Looking sideways at him through her fingers.*) Accuse me, of trying to pull Lord Poverty's— limb.

Jack. — Helen, you know I love you. (*Approaching her again.*)

Helen. — You don't! (*Retreating.*) You never have? (*Going to left entrance.*) And you can see, that I'm not dying for you. (*Exit Helen.*)

Jack. — (*With an air of satisfaction.*) This is business! Love—real love—true love—seasoned now and then with a little misunderstanding is heaven; but constant scraping, peppered at long intervals, with too much love is— (*Pauses.*) I imagine—(*Looking toward front entrance and taking a cigar from his pocket.*) I'll go out and take a smoke, then I'll come back and brace the old man; tell him everything, everything. (*Exit through front entrance. Enters Poverty.*

Poverty. — (*Reflects.*) Me shares. (*Enters Helen.*)

Helen. — Now is a good time to tell father that the great art critic is no other than Jack Robins Jr. that he wants to marry me—that he is awfully smart—that he's madly in love with me and things like that. Don't tell Jack!

Poverty. — Of course—things like that. (*Exit Helen through front hallway. Enters Rushfoot.*)

Rushfoot. — Well Poverty, my boy! how are you, anyway? The devil take that dueling affair? Do you know, I havn't had a minute with you, alone, since the Prince's visit.

Poverty. — How did the celebration come off?

Rushfoot. — I'm awfully sorry you were n't there. 'Twas great! The Prince acted like a perfect gentleman. In his speech he said that the principal of arbitration was right—that the edicts of an impartial tribunal was preferable, to the distressing judgments of the battle field, and so on and so forth. He was very nice. Then I spoke! My boy, I was in great form. Following Wales, I said that my country and his should join hands forever—but here was my most eloquent outburst. "The most perfect union in all nature, transcending the union of states, or the compact of empires—a union compared with which, the espousals of heaven, or the wedlocks of earth w re but robes of sands—and that combination w. s — the union of the Siamese Twins. To these, inseparable fragments of humanity, nature pointed with indexed significance to the great possibilities of a real Anglo-American combine, with one flag, bearing upon it's folds, the imperishable motto " Arbitration and Free Trade for England—Forever!" My dear boy, the American ambassador, why, he just wept with joy!

Poverty — Fancy! You know your daughter Helen—

Rushfoot. — I should say so.

Poverty. — Of course, why not? You see, she'll be marriageable soon.

Rushfoot. — She' old enough now.

Poverty. — Old enough—of cou se—but you see, it's quite the thing to let a girl know her fate for a year or two. She's in love.

Rushfoot. — Well! How about you?

Poverty. — Me? (*Looking at* Rushfoot.) I don't mind telling you; the maggot is at me heart too·

Rushfoot. — It won't do Poverty. (*To himself.*) I'm sorry.

Poverty. — Your permission is all that's—

Rushfoot. — (*Sorrowfully.*) Now Poverty, I like you, you're a descendant of the old barons: I like the children of the old baron, though those medieval scamps, swore, swaggered, and swined in times of peace—yet in the hour of peril, they forged to the front, clear up to the vizor of their enimies, smote them down or fell themselves. That's right! Sure!

Poverty. — About Helen, you see the girl has been hoodwinking—

Rushfoot. — (*Interrupting.*) No she hasn't, I've heard a few things' Now, how are you fixed?

Poverty. — How am I fixed?

Rushfoot. — Yes.

Poverty. — Oh! me assets—if you've any interest in knowing, I don't mind telling you, I have an estate in Scotland.

Rushfoot. — Does this belong to you?

Poverty. — Poverty Castle?

Rushfoot. — Yes.

Poevrty. — I've only a life interest in it. I have an estate in Scotland, a few miles of dirt and rocks, and old trees that have been groaning away for five hundred years. Then there's the stone.

Rushfoot. — A quarry?

Poverty. — No. the rocks of the castle. Some bridge building chaps offer to buy the stone.

Rushfoot. — (*Earnestly.*) Don't tear the castle down— why, sell it!

Poverty. — Could I now?

Rushfoot. — Sure if you can manage to throw in a title with the rocks.

Poverty. — A title goes with the jail.

Rushfoot. — Jail! I thought it was a castle?

Poverty. — A castle—of course to be sure; but you see, me great, great grandfather leased it as a jail, or mad house once—and there's me three thousand shares—

Rushfoot. — (*Interrupting.*) If a title goes with the castle, you can sell it to any widow in New York, among the four hundred. It don't matter, my boy, whether it's

a castle, jail or lunatic asylum; if the title gives
the dear old girl the right to sit even on the royal
woodpile, and look into the Queen's kitchen. (*Helen
appears in front hallway walking on tiptoes. On reaching
front entrance, beckons* Poverty. *The latter makes an excuse to approach* Helen, *just as* Rushfoot *finishes his last
speech* Helen *whispers to* Poverty.)

Poverty. - (*To* Helen.) We havn't got to the point
yet.

Helen. — (*To* Poverty.) Make way for Jack then, he's
coming to the front like a man. (Helen *disappears*.)

Poverty. — (*To* Rushfoot.) Of course—to be sure.
(*Putting his hand in his pocket, as though searching for a
paper.*) Pardon me a moment, I had an inventory of me
assets. Where can it be? (*Goes to left entrance.*) Just a
moment. *Exit* Poverty.)

Rushfoot. — (*Shaking his head.*) No—England claims
one child, she shall have only one; yet Poverty is a
good fellow. (*Helen and* Jack *appear in the hallway*,
Helen *kisses him, while he straightens up preparatory to his
interview with* Rushfoot. *Enters* Jack.)

Jack. — (*Coughing*.) Mr. Rushfoot. (*With nervous
dignity.*)

Rushfoot. — Why Randolph! how are you? (*Takes
Jack's hand.* Helen *is seen peeping around the corner of left
pillar.*)

Jack. — Randolph is not my—name.

Rushfoot. — (*Aside.*) What impertinence! (*To Jack
snappishly.*) Mr. Randolph, does that suit you better?

Jack. — No, no, Mr. Rushfoot, you don't understand
me. My full name is, John Jack—Ran—dolph. (*Disgusted with himself.*)

Rushfoot. — Oh, I see! (*Laughing.*) You take no
exception to Randolph.

Jack. — No sir. I trust that some day, you will do
me the honor of calling me your so—your Jack—just
Jack—ordinary Jack—just Randolph Jack (*Aside.*) This
is tough!

Rushfoot. — (*Laughing and shaking head.*) Sure! I

had a friend named Jack once, Jack - (*Reflecting*.) Robins. We were boys together. He was the wildest devil I ever knew, and they tell me, that he's got a son that's a terror.

Jack. — How did your friend Jack Robins pan out?

Rushfoot. — (*Deliberately*.) Oh, all right as a man, but as a boy—My heavens! Cheek! He had an effulgent front, that would make a horse shy.

Jack. — Have you ever seen his son?

Rushfoot. — No, nor I don't want to! (Helen *in despair*.) But Jack, how are you, you are also an art critic?

Jack. — (*Aside*.) I'll give him a sample off my effulgent front. (*To* Rushfoot.) Art critic, yes sir,—an art critic, that's what I pretend to be. I'm clever and ambitious.

Rushfoot. — That's good, that's the way to talk. (*Aside*.) Just a little gall. (*To* Jack.) Ambitious, that's right.

Jack. — Ambitious to get married.

Rushfoot. — Why don't you?

Jack. — With your permission, I will.

Rushfoot. — (*Surprised*.) My permission?

Jack. — Yes, Mr. Rushfoot, with your consent, I'll marry your lovely daughter. Helen is anxious, and I'm willing, no, no, the anxiety is here! (*Pointing to himself*.)

Rushfoot. — (*With surpressed indignation*.) Have you been making love to my daughter, sir?

Jack. — (*Earnestly and looking* Rushfoot *in the face*.) I have. J'm a man of taste.

Rushfoot. — (*Cooling down*.) Admirable taste, but— (*Enters* Poverty, Rushfoot *looks at* Poverty *and then at* Jack. *Aside*.) Great Scott! how many more! This makes three, counting that young schamp in America, Jack Robins.

Poverty. — I cant find me inventory.

Rushfoot. — Never mind, my lord.

Poverty. — (*Looking at* Rushfoot *and then at* Jack.) Am I in the way?

Jack. — Not in my way.

Poverty. — That's it.

Rushfoot. — (*To* Poverty.) Do you know, that Mr. Randolph is also in love with my daughter?

Jack. — (*To himself—surprised.*) Also in love?

Poverty. — I don't know about the also chap, but I do know about Jack, he wants to take Helen over.

Rushfoot. — Take her over?

Poverty. — Yes—marry her— why not?

Rushfoot. — (*Looking at* Jack, *and then at* Poverty *aside.*) This is mysterious! (*To* Poverty.) Not five minutes ago, you were asking my consent—

Poverty. — To be sure—to let Jack have her.

Rushfoot. — (*Aside.*) Oh, that's different! There's one third of the mystery solved.

Jack. — I didn't ask anybody to intercede in my behalf, I'm man enough to face the music myself.

Rushfoot. — I think you are. (*Aside.*) I'll floor him! (*To* Jack.) As uming that you're a gentleman, and not addicted to the use of brandy, I'll discuss this question, evan in the presence of his lordship. When my daughter marries, I shall give her two hundred thousand dollars in addition to her own fortune. What will you give her?

Jack. — Two hundred and one thousand.

Rushfoot. — Are you a young man of fortune?

Jack. — I'll cover your money and raise you one.

Rushfoot. — Who are you anyway?

Jack. — John Randolph Robins, Jr.

Rushfoot. — (*Looking at* Jack.) So you are, and a chip of the old block. (*Surveying him.*) So you're Jack Robin's son?

Poverty. — Of course—the art critic.

Rushfoot. — (*Aside.*) Two thirds of the mystery is cleared up. Well, well, well. (*To* Jack.) You'll permit me a little breathing spell, won't you.

Poverty. — (*To* Jack, *pleadingly*.) Of course—why not?

Jack. — A short one, yes.

Rushfoot. — (*Going toward left entrance*.) Is it possible? (*Looks at* Jack.) Yes, the other third of the mystery vanishes. (*Exit* Rushfoot.)

Helen. — (*Enters from arched entrance*.) Come on Jack.

Jack. — Hurrah! (*To* Poverty.) Come on, let's get out of here. Hurrah!

Poverty. — Why not? (*Exeunt* Jack, Helen *and* Poverty. Helen *and* Jack *are seen embracing*. Poverty *congratulating them*. *Enters* Mr. Maby *followed by* Mrs. Maby.)

Maby. — Her treachery was fiendish—she ought to suffer.

Mrs. Maby. — She does. Read her letter.

Maby. — (*Refusing letter*.) No, no! Forget her.

Mrs. Maby. — She has left Dorchester Oaks for good, —London is to be her future home. Poor sinful Lizzie, gone out of my life forever! No friends and poor Even Mr. Gower en learning of her treacherous letter to the London press broke their engagement and refused even to see her.

Maby. — Come, let us wander through the labyrinths of this historical old place. (*Exeunt* Mr. *and* Mrs. Maby. *Enters* Helen *and* Effie *through main hallway, the latter laughing half hysterically*.)

Helen. — (*Out of breath. Laughs*.) Oh, how Jack did mix us all up!

Effie. — You and Jack are mixed up for good now, aren't you? (*Laughing*.) Oh dear!

Helen. — (*Sentimentally*.) Forever and forever! Father hasn't said the word yet, but it's all right. I must get a wrap, Jack made me come back ond get one. He's so careful of me. (*To* Effie.) Why don't you get engaged it's so nice? Do please, for my sake.

Effie. — (*Laughing*.) For your sake?

Helen. — (*Earnestly.*) I mean for Lord Poverty's sake. He loves you, and he's got money now. Of course, I wouldn't sacrifice you to a lord, unless he had money—of course not.

Effie. — You think he loves me?

Helen. — I *know* he does! (*Tragically.*) I swear he does! (*Looking at Effie with a knowing glance.*) And I know something more than that.

Effie. — What, pray?

Helen. — You love him. (*Tragically.*) I'll swear to that too.

Effie. — (*Seriously. 'Putting her arm around* Helen.) ou happy, happy, dear girl! I will tell you. Though Lord Poverty is a strange man, different from all men, in all ways, I do love him. He sought me, a poor girl, forced by fate to abide in a land, and among a people, that my father, my mother knew not; he has asked me to become his wife. Helen, I would, if Bruce Buckingham were here to give—his consent, for I d - I do love him. I have tried to laugh the thought out of my life, but in vain. Some mysterious, undefinable influence tells me, that I shall be his wife, but not until Bruce Buckingham consents. (*Making an effort to laugh.*) So you see I shall have to wait.

Helen. — Does Lord Poverty know you are only waiting?

Effie. — (*Shaking her head.*) No!

Helen. — Here he comes. Oh, Jack will scold for keeping him waiting so long. (*Exit* Helen. *Enters* Poverty.)

Poverty. — You're alone Miss Revere? You see I must call you that hereafter—of course—why not?

Effie. — Please don't Lord Poverty.

Poverty. — Some day, when you're married, I might call you Maloney, when your husband was about; it would be awkward, you know.

Effie. — I shall never marry.

Poverty. — You we n't now, Fancy!

Effie. — Never!

Poverty. — (*Looking at* Effie.) You will make a good spinster? Some day, in years to come. (*Rings.*) Of course—why not? You've been a fine girl, Maloney—I've had me eye on you. And you want to be a spinster?

E fie. — Yes, an old maid.

Poverty. — The world thinks, that any sort of feminine rubbish is good enough for a wife, that an old maid is good for nothing. They forget, that in the matrimonial market, the best stuff is often left over. It gets shop worn, why not?—but the quality is there. (*Enters* Bullock. *To* Bullock.) Bullock fetch me *old* assets.

Bullock. — Himmediately, me lud. (Bullock *retires.*)

Effie. — The same holds true of bachelors, does it not?

Poverty. — Why not?

Effie. — You'll marry some time, my lord.

Poverty. — (*Looking at* Effie *with marked earnestness.*) If I wait until you're shop worn, will you have me? Of course – you might chance me then.

E fie. — (*Bashfully.*) How long are you to be in America?

Poverty. — (*Turning his head slowly and looking at* Effie *in slight astonishment.*) Not till you're shop worn You've color enough in your face to last for years—wrinkles don't come in a day. I'll come back - why not? and wait for years—and watch you decay. You might have a bad spell for a year or two. of course—then you'd wear quick. You know a woman without beauty, is like a soldier without a gun. She surrenders at the word. I'll knock about alone —(*Looking at* Effie.) until your cheeks fade.

Effie. — Lord Poverty, I believe you love me.

Poverty. — Why not? You see I've always been—(*To himself*) mushed—mushed—that's not it—squashed—yes—that's it. I've always—(*Hesitates.*) wanted you.

Effie. — (*Approaches* Poverty. *Solemnly and with eyes fixed on the floor.*) Lord Poverty, I love you. Though I love you, I can not become your wife without the con-

sent—(*Enters* Bullock *carrying old steamer trunk. On the
end, painted in black letters, is the name* " Bruce Buckingham" *sticking out front beneath the cover, is a quantity of
straw. As* Bullock *approaches the table, where he places the
trunk, the straw falls on to the floor.*

Bullock. — Me lud, Hi'ad to clear haway the rubbish. When Hi placed the trunk hin the Harches Tower,
Hi must 'ave left the top hup, me lud.

Poverty. — (*Opening the trunk, and slowly wiping his
hands with handkerchief.*) You left the top up, of course.
The straw from the rack above has been falling on me
assets.

Effie. — (*Aside.*) I must control my feelings. I have
for months and I shall continue to. I'll laugh; yes,
laugh. (*Struggling with her emotions. To* Poverty.) Do
you keep your valuables in the stable?

Poverty. — No, in the tower. I've lost the only
valuable assets I had. If they're not here, there no
where. (*Opens the trunk.* Effie *approaches the table,*
Poverty *takes straw out and throws it on the floor.* Poverty
looks into the trunk with an odd gaze. Effie *starts.*) Here
Bullock—(*Taking a* cat *from the trunk.*) you needn't mind
the other cat.

Bullock. - (*Who has been picking up straw from floor.*)
Very well, me lud. (_ akes cat and goes to left entrance.*)

Effie. — (*Laughing.*) Is that one of your valuable
assets?

Poverty. — (*Taking* kittens *from the trunk.*) Bullock!

Bullock. — Yes, me lud. (*Turns; trys to conceal a
broad smile on seeing the kittens. Approaches* Poverty.)

Poverty. — Be careful of the cat. (*Hands* Bullock
kittens.)

Bullock. — Yes, me lud.

Poverty. — It's the only asset I've got, that pays a
dividend. (Bullock *retires with cat and kittens.*)

Effie. — (*Who has been taken with a fit of uncontrolable
laughter.*) Oh dear! Pardon me! (*Continues to laugh.
Goes to front entrance greatly embarrassed.*)

Poverty. — (*Looking at* Effie) You see the cat and kittens were not the assets I was after. (*Looks in trunk.*) What's this? (*Takes bundle of papers from trunk.*) Here are me shares—(*Examining different documents.*) I think so—I'm (*Looks at paper.*) not—yes, here they are. (*To* Effie.) You said you couldn't become me wife, unless some one consented.

Effie. — (*Who still laughs, and in evident distress. Nods.*) Yes. (*Laughs.*)

Poverty. — (*With shares in hand, looks at* Effie.) Who's the chap? (*Shuts down cover of trunk.*)

Effie. — (*Who sees the name* " Bruce Buckingham " *on end of trunk, still laughing, now hysterically. Poverty takes her by the hand. Effie half unconsciously staggers to the trunk, throws herself on it.*) Bruce Buckingham! (*Now weeping and laughing.*)

Poverty. — (*To* Bullock, *who appears at left entrance, looking for more straw.*) Brandy!

Bullock. - Yes me lud. (*Bullock retires.*)

Poverty. — (*Leads* Effie *to a sofa.*) Sit down—why not? (*Aside.*) They tell me a shock is good for hysteria. (*Kisses her. To* Effie) I'm Bruce Buckingham. (*Aside.*) An other shock, (*Kisses her again.*) I consent.

Effie. — (*Starts.*) What?

Poverty. — It's your medicine. (*Enters* Bullock *with brandy bottle and a glass. Poverty pours some into a glass offers it to* Effie.) It's brandy. (*Effie drinks.*)

Effie. — (*Standing up.*) Oh! (*Looks at* Poverty.) You Bruce Buckingham?

Poverty. — Of course—why not?

Effie. — (*Throws her arms around* Poverty's *neck.*) Bruce Buckingham. (*Kisses him.*)

Poverty. — (*Kisses* Effie *and looks at audience.*) Why not; (*To* Effie.) I'll tell you all about it, when we get on the steamer.

Effie. — Steamer?

Poverty. — Yes, you're going to America with us. You see, my full name, cutting off a yard at each end, is

Bruce Courtland, Phellps, Buckingham, Poverty. (*Enter* Helen *and* Jack.)

Helen. — (*Seeing* Poverty *with his arm supporting* Effie.) Oh, have you—?

Effie. — (*Approaches trunk and leans against it.*) Yes.

Poverty. — (*To* Helen·) Yes, I'm to take her over.

Helen. — (*Clapping her hands.*) I'm so happy! (*To* Poverty.) She loved you all the time. (*To* Effie, *kissing her.*) You see, Jack, I wasn't pulling his foot—for a title. (Jack *smiles,* Helen *laughs.*)

Jack. — (*Shakes* Poverty's *hand.*) Here comes a lucky man.

Helen. — (*Who sees her father approaching the left entrance.*) Lucky?

Jack. — Yes, to get me for a son-in-law. (*To* Rushfoot, *who is followed by* Mr. *and* Mrs. Maby.) How about that breathing spell?

Rushfoot. — I've had it. Every one in this Castle is your friend, and I am too. (*Shakes* Jack's *hand.*) Look here, twas that brandy that did it. You had a good chance to play the goody, goody sneak, and you didn't. Jack (*In a low voice.*) let me off for a hundred thousand wont you?

Jack. — Ask Helen.

Rushfoot. — (*Putting his arm around* Helen.) You will wont you?

Helen. — (*Looks at* Jack *who shakes his head.*) Father I can't.

Rushfoot. — Well children, God bless you!

Mrs. Maby. — (*Laughing and kissing* Jack.) I never dreamed of having a great art critic for a brother.

Maby. — (*To all.*) Harry rode over a moment ago and brought the news " Sirao pleaded guilty, and got five years " Maxey is doing well and clapped his hands for joy, when he heard that he was to go back to Italy, and that I had made an arrangments to support and educate him. The papers say I am be knighted.

All. — Good, good!

Rushfoot. — (*To* Poverty, *who has been talking to* Effie. *Low music*, Life on the Ocean wave.) Well Bruce my boy we're off. And you're going to marry? That's right, sure! Be happy, live in peace and in America.

Poverty. — Of course. You see, if Maloney and I have any misunderstanding, we'll submit the thing to arbitration.

Rushfoot. — That's right! Let *your* motto be " Maloney and Poverty—for Maloney—Forever."

Poverty. — Of course. (*To* Rushfoot.) I'll sell me castle in Scotland.

Rushfoot. — Your jail. (*Laughing*.)

Poverty. — Of course. Sell me jail to the four hundred New York widows, and live in America.

Effie. -- Yes, beneath the blue skies.

Poverty. -- Of course—why not?

— THE END —

TABLE

GENEVA. -- PRINTING OFFICE HAUSSMANN & ZŒLLNER
3, RUE DU MONT-BLANC, 3